DISNEP

JASMINE'S
QUEST
··for the··
STARDUST
SAPPHIRE

DISNEP

JASMINE'S QUEST
for the
STARDUST SAPPHIRE

By Kathy McCullough

Illustrated by Lindsay Dale-Scott

Random House 🏠 New York

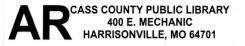

For all young adventurers

rhcbooks.com
ISBN 978-0-7364-3962-6 (trade) — ISBN 978-0-7364-8273-8 (lib. bdg.)
Printed in the United States of America
10 9 8 7 6 5 4 3 2 1

Prologue

On a beautiful moonless night, a falling star soared over the kingdom of Agrabah. Sparkling streaks of color followed the star, creating a shimmering rainbow that illuminated the sky.

In the desert below, sand swirled, kicked up by a sudden gust of wind. Within moments, the twinkling colors had faded from view....

CHAPTER 1

In the game room of the palace, Princess Jasmine reached toward the chessboard to move one of her pieces. Her father, the Sultan of Agrabah, sat across from her. "Don't be hasty," he warned. "Playing board games is like ruling a kingdom. You need to think several steps ahead and consider all the options. You must be certain each move you make is the best choice."

"I *think* it's the best choice," said Jasmine.

"Well then, go ahead!" The Sultan smiled and gestured for her to make her move.

But Jasmine was no longer sure. She frowned and studied the board.

"I like games of speed," said Aladdin, who stood next to the table watching. Abu, his pet monkey, chittered in agreement from his shoulder. Aladdin picked up a knight that had been captured earlier in the game and tapped it along the edge of the table, as if the tiny horse figurine were running. "Speed and *chance*." He smiled and snatched up two other captured pieces.

Aladdin was a former street thief, but he had given up his life of crime after falling in love with Jasmine, and he now lived in the palace. However, he had not lost his fondness for action and excitement. "Speed, chance, and *tricks*!" he continued. Aladdin tossed the pieces into the air and juggled them. Behind him, the closed drapes fluttered below their sashes, muting the howl of the evening winds outside.

"I'm trying to concentrate!" protested Jasmine, struggling not to laugh at Aladdin's antics. She returned her focus to the board. She'd been playing board games all her life, but when she was growing up, they had been just for fun. Now the Sultan encouraged her to play to sharpen her mind, using them to teach her lessons about leadership, since she would one day take over for him and become the ruler of Agrabah. As a result, the games had become serious and important—a way to practice strategy for the life-or-death decisions she'd be making in the future.

After considering all her possible moves, Jasmine picked up a bishop and moved it three spaces. The Sultan beamed at Jasmine. "Good move!" he said before allowing a sly smile. "But you did not think *quite* far enough ahead." He slid his queen up the board, capturing Jasmine's bishop and giving the queen a direct line to her king.

"*Oooh,*" said Aladdin, not really understanding what the move meant but knowing the

Sultan had bested Jasmine somehow. Jasmine had tried to teach Aladdin the rules, but he liked to make up his own as they went along. That made it a lot more interesting, as far as he was concerned. No staring at the board for hours and hours. Keep it moving and make it lively! What was the point of a game if it wasn't fun?

Jasmine groaned, frustrated. What had she done wrong? How had she failed to predict her father's move? If only she'd made a different choice, her king would not be in danger of being checkmated. Every match she lost underscored her growing nervousness about leading the kingdom one day.

Jasmine had never truly had her leadership skills tested. She had helped Aladdin and Genie defeat Jafar, the Sultan's evil advisor, who had tried to take control of the kingdom, but she had acted on instinct then, rather than strategy. She desperately wanted to prove to her father— and herself—that when the time came, she would be worthy and capable of ruling Agrabah.

Abu, bored with the game, leapt onto the table and snatched Jasmine's king.

"Abu!" cried Jasmine as the little monkey dashed toward the window with the piece.

"I'll get him," said Aladdin, but before he could take a step, a powerful breeze blew the drapes free of their sashes and lifted Abu off the ground. Abu shrieked in terror and landed in Aladdin's arms as wind and sand swirled around the room.

Aladdin spotted a blue four-pointed star in the sky, glowing beneath the dim light of the moon. Before he could study it more closely, sand blew into his eyes, temporarily blinding him.

"Close the drapes!" the Sultan called. Aladdin blinked away the sand and grabbed one side of the thick velvet curtains as Abu clung tightly to him. Jasmine rushed over and grabbed the other side, shielding her face with one arm. Together, she and Aladdin pulled the drapes closed.

But fierce gusts continued to batter the drapes,

causing them to billow inward. The wind thumped and roared, like a monster trying to break in.

Abu shook the sand out of his fur. Jasmine combed her fingers through her hair, loosening more sand, which pooled at her feet.

Aladdin, meanwhile, stood still, thinking. "Did you see that?" he asked Jasmine. "That blue shape in the sky?"

"All I could see was sand blowing around," said Jasmine. She turned to her father. "It's been like this for days. I know there are sometimes sand-storms out in the desert, but I don't remember anything this bad ever hitting the city for so long, with no break."

"I don't either," said the Sultan, brushing sand out of his white beard. "Our windy season is in winter, which is still months away. Spring usually has calm winds."

Aladdin moved to the window and pulled back the edge of one curtain to peer out.

"Stop!" protested Jasmine. "You'll let in more sand!"

"I just wanted to see if it's still there." Aladdin squinted through a slim gap in the drapes, but the view was now obscured by sand, the sky dark and hazy. He was certain he had seen it, though. "It was so strange," he said. "It had a blue tint to it, and four points."

"That sounds like the clay star on the arch over the gates into Agrabah," said Jasmine as she brushed more sand off the chessboard.

"It *did* kind of look like that star," said Aladdin. "But the arch is on the opposite side of the city from where this window faces. The star I saw was out over the desert." A gust of sandy wind snuck through the opening in the drapes and Aladdin pulled them closed.

"That reminds me of an old nursery rhyme," said the Sultan with a wistful smile. "*Do you see the star shine? Do you hear the winds blow? . . .* I don't remember the rest of it."

"I do," said Aladdin. He knotted the sashes together. "When I lived on the streets, my friends and I used to sing it to tease each other." He hummed to himself for a few seconds, remembering the tune, and then began to sing:

"Do you see the blue star shine?
Do you hear the fierce winds blow?
It's a sign—
You're out of time.
Quick! You must restore the pieces,
Or endure a storm that never ceases. . . ."

"Pieces of what?" asked Jasmine when he had finished.

Aladdin shrugged. "I don't know. It's just an old song. I never really thought about what it meant."

At that moment, the sashes gave up their fight with the wind and the curtains blew free. As

Jasmine and Aladdin rushed to close them again, Jasmine saw it: a glowing blue star in the sky. It shone down through the violent, twisting clouds of sand, as if trying to cast a spotlight on something below.

And then, as quickly as it came, the image was gone, lost behind the swirling sand.

CHAPTER 2

Jasmine and Aladdin went to the royal library early the next morning to look for clues to help them solve the mystery of the winds. Jasmine searched the towering shelves that lined the room for books dealing with the history of Agrabah. She hoped she could find evidence that the winds were not as unusual as she feared and would soon pass. While Abu entertained himself by climbing along the highest shelves, Aladdin gathered several volumes of myths and legends.

Jasmine and Aladdin took seats at opposite ends of a long table. "You should be helping me look through these," said Jasmine, indicating her history books, "instead of reading made-up tales. This wind is really happening, and we need to find *real* information about it." The curtains in front of the library's shuttered windows fluttered, as if to echo Jasmine's words.

"The tales were inspired by something," replied Aladdin. He knew from experience that myths often contained more truth than many people gave them credit for. "For instance, there are plenty of stories about genies in here."

"That's true," agreed Jasmine. "But it's impossible to know what's real and what's not in those old legends." She paged through the book in front of her, moving backward through Agrabah's history, from the present into the past. She reached the beginning of the previous century but still found nothing. The weather in the kingdom seemed to have always been comfortably mild. Rain was light and lasted only long enough to water the desert plants. Winds came and went, serving to blow away detritus and smooth out the desert's sands. Lightning was sometimes seen high up in the mountain regions, but the flashes stayed in the clouds and never hit the earth.

Jasmine turned another page, arriving at a chapter filled with illustrations of different parts of the city, including the royal palace and the marketplace. She spotted a drawing of the towering gates to the city and their soaring arch— but there was no clay star in the gate then as there was now. Instead, there was just a big gap in the arch's peak. She skimmed the text below the illustration for information. It stated that a giant star-shaped sapphire had once occupied the spot in the peak.

"A star-shaped *sapphire*?" Jasmine said to herself, confused. She thought the clay star in the arch had always been there. This was the first she had heard about a sapphire.

Aladdin looked up from his book. "Did you find something?" he asked.

"It says here that the star over the gates to Agrabah was originally a giant sapphire, but that it was destroyed at one point," said Jasmine. "The spot was left empty for several decades, and the sapphire was eventually replaced by the clay star we have now."

"That's strange," said Aladdin.

Jasmine shook her head. "This can't be true. It also says the original sapphire was destroyed by a gulin. Everybody knows gulin aren't real. They're just monsters from scary stories." Gulin sometimes popped up in the fairy-tale books she had read as a child. They were spooky, green-tinted wraiths with the ability to shape-shift into any animal or human form, usually for evil purposes.

"But there they are in your *history* book," Aladdin pointed out. Abu hopped onto Aladdin's shoulder and nodded in agreement.

Jasmine found it hard to argue this. "If only

Genie were here," she said. "He might know what really happened."

"Unless he was trapped in his lamp at the time," said Aladdin. "Anyway, the last message we got from him said he was still traveling. There's no way to know where he is now."

"You're right," said Jasmine. "We're going to have to figure this out on our own."

"There's a whole book of gulin legends here somewhere. . . ." Aladdin sifted through the stack of books he had taken off the shelves. "Found it!" He picked up an old volume with a worn cover and flipped it open to the table of contents. Abu leapt from Aladdin's shoulder onto the table and followed Aladdin's finger as it moved down the titles.

"Aha!" said Aladdin.

Jasmine joined Aladdin and Abu, and she read the title aloud: "'The Sand God and the Sapphire.'"

Aladdin turned to the right page and pointed at the colorful illustration opposite the first page of the tale. It was another drawing of the Agrabah city gates, but this time with a brilliant blue star-shaped sapphire in the arch.

"*The Sand God wove the sapphire from the dust of a falling star,*" Aladdin read aloud. "*This fallen star was made of magic gathered over millions of years. The Sand God gifted the sapphire to the founders of Agrabah, promising it would keep the atmosphere of the kingdom and its surroundings in a state of balance so that its citizens could flourish.*"

The story went on to tell about how an evil gulin had climbed up to the arch, pulled the sapphire free, and tossed it onto the stone path below out of spite. The gem shattered into four pieces, which instantly vanished.

Jasmine pointed to the next passage and read: "*The magic that had preserved Agrabah's stable climate was destroyed, triggering a curse with the potential to spread deadly weather throughout the kingdom, unless the pieces were found and returned to the Sand God to restore.*" She looked up at Aladdin. "That nursery rhyme you and Father were talking about yesterday," she said. "It mentioned 'pieces'—and a blue star, remember?"

Aladdin's eyes went wide. "And 'fierce winds.'"

"And how you have to 'restore the pieces, or—'"

Aladdin met Jasmine's eyes. "'Endure a storm that never ceases . . . ,'" he finished.

"Could it be?" Jasmine asked, mystified by the possibility. "Could the winds we're experiencing have something to do with the shattered sapphire?"

"If the sapphire *was* magic, and it really kept the weather in balance—it makes sense," said Aladdin.

"The sapphire was destroyed centuries ago, though," said Jasmine. "Why would the winds have only started now?"

"We haven't finished the story." Aladdin turned the page. "Look. Here it is. *The Sand God used his magic to delay the instability and chaos for a thousand years. To signal when the thousand years was nearly up, the Sand God would fling a star through the sky, with a* tail that sparkled with every color of the rainbow.'"

Jasmine gasped. "Remember that falling star we saw last week? It sent out all those colors—just like it says in the story!"

Jasmine and Aladdin had been out on her balcony. There was no moon, and the sky shimmered with millions of twinkling stars. Aladdin was singing Jasmine a new song he had just written when a gorgeous burst of light had rocketed across the sky, creating a glittering arc of different hues, like a nighttime rainbow.

Jasmine also remembered the breeze that had followed. It had come up as soon as the last of the colorful sparks had faded from the sky. At first it was pleasant, but it quickly grew in force, and Jasmine and Aladdin had been chased inside.

"The winds have continued since then," she told Aladdin.

He nodded. "And they've gotten worse."

As if summoned by Aladdin's words, a fierce

gust of wind hit the shutters, which banged open, ripping the sash over the curtains. Wind swirled into the room, causing the pages of the books to flap violently. As Jasmine and Aladdin ran to close the shutters, the book of gulin tales was blown to the floor.

Abu hopped down from the table to the book. He bounced up and down next to it, pointing to the open page and chittering excitedly.

"What is it, Abu?" Jasmine asked as she hurried over to him. She picked up the book. Aladdin walked over and joined them. "It's the last page of the legend," she said. Most of the page was filled with a drawing of the moon. It glowed brightly yet eerily in a completely black sky. There was just one line of text at the top of the page. Jasmine read, "'If the pieces of the sapphire were not retrieved by the time the first full moon reached its zenith after the rainbow comet fell, all would be lost.'"

Aladdin moved to a calendar posted on the wall. "The next full moon . . ." He searched the calendar and then stopped, finding what he was looking for. He turned to Jasmine, meeting her eyes, and said, "The next full moon is only three days away."

CHAPTER 3

Jasmine and Aladdin immediately left the library and found the Sultan in his throne room. Jasmine had brought the history book and the collection of gulin legends to show her father as she explained what she and Aladdin had found out.

"But there is no such thing as gulin," said the Sultan.

"Maybe so," said Jasmine. "But the original star in the arch did break. These drawings in the history book prove it. And these winds are very real, as was whatever we saw in the sky." The strange blue star-shaped glow over the desert was a piece of the puzzle they did not yet understand. The legend hadn't mentioned anything about it, but the fact that it resembled the illustration of the original sapphire suggested that it was connected somehow. "We need to at least go out to the desert to look," Jasmine told her father. "The pieces of the broken sapphire may be there. If we can find them and put them back together, maybe the winds will stop."

"It's too dangerous out there, Jasmine," said the Sultan.

"We'll be careful, Father," Jasmine assured him. "We can take Magic Carpet. I promise we'll come right back if we don't find anything."

The captain of the royal guard entered the room. "Your Highness," he said. "We've received more reports of injuries in the marketplace."

The Sultan let out a tense sigh and his black eyebrows furrowed in concern. "The time has come," he said with a frown. "We need to close the marketplace, for everyone's safety."

Aladdin and Jasmine exchanged a look. Shutting the market meant cutting people off from their access to food and preventing the vendors from earning their living.

The Sultan knew this as well and had already thought ahead. "Assemble a team of guards to deliver food and water to the citizens until the winds have calmed," he told the captain. The captain started for the door. "Wait," said the Sultan, summoning him back. "We'll also need to set up a shelter with medical care available for those who need it." He thought a moment. "The old stables behind the palace," he said at last. "Have another team of guards clear it out. Have it ready by dawn tomorrow."

The captain nodded in acknowledgment and hurried out.

Jasmine stared at her father, amazed at how quickly he had devised a strategy—and how confidently he had issued the orders. It was as if he had no doubts at all.

The Sultan crossed to his desk and began jotting down notes. "As soon as I make sure the guards have carried out my orders, I'll get ready." He glanced over at Jasmine. "If this star really exists, it is I who must go to the desert, my dear. I can't risk losing you to these deadly winds."

Jasmine rushed to the Sultan's side. "No, Father. You have to stay here. You are Agrabah's ruler. Your people need you, especially now."

"You are the *future* ruler, don't forget," said the Sultan.

"As the future ruler, this is how I can help," insisted Jasmine. "You can then assure the people we are doing everything we can—and that a solution to the winds may have already been found. I can do this, Father," Jasmine pleaded. "Please have faith in me."

The Sultan took Jasmine's hands in his. "I do, my child. Never have any doubt of that. Always remember, I am your biggest fan!"

Aladdin coughed pointedly. The Sultan raised his eyebrows and gave Aladdin a wry smile. "I know you feel the same, young man. But as a parent, I get to claim first place in this contest."

Aladdin nodded to the Sultan as if to agree— but then peered over at Jasmine and pointed to himself, mouthing, *"Number-one fan."*

Jasmine stifled a laugh. She was glad for a light moment in the midst of all that was happening.

Later that afternoon, Jasmine and Aladdin each packed a bag of supplies and headed out. They had arranged to meet Magic Carpet at the gates to Agrabah, where the city walls would provide a buffer from the winds, making it a safer place to begin their flight. Jasmine squinted through the gap in the scarf she'd wrapped around her face underneath her cloak. She could see the top of Abu's head peeking out from under Aladdin's cloak.

As they made their way through the city streets, Jasmine was able to witness firsthand the destruction the winds had caused. Vendor carts were toppled, their contents strewn about. Shards of broken pottery and bits of shredded tapestries blew past their feet.

When they reached the gates, the sun had just begun to set, causing the blowing sand to take on a golden glow. Jasmine glanced up toward the clay star in the arch. "I hope all four pieces of the sapphire *are* out there," she said. She felt certain that going into the desert was the right move—but she hadn't thought beyond this. She did not yet have a strategy.

As she spoke, a new image came into view: a beautiful indigo and crimson tapestry with four golden tassels soaring over the city's walls. Images of fierce tigers were woven into the design near each corner, but there was nothing menacing about the playful carpet, who performed a couple of loop the loops as he flew down past the arch. He landed vertically in front of Jasmine and Aladdin, poised on two tassels.

"Magic Carpet," said Jasmine with a smile, charmed as she always was by their spirited friend. "Thank you for helping us."

Carpet dipped a tassel, as if to say, *It's my pleasure.* He performed one final flip and then spread out horizontally, hovering about a foot above the ground. He lowered his front end to allow Jasmine and Aladdin to step on.

As Magic Carpet rose up, Abu noticed a meerkat lurking in the shadows of the city's gates. The animal's head was cocked, its expression curious, almost as if it had been listening to the conversation. It stepped into the dim light, revealing the strange green tint of its fur.

Magic Carpet sailed out toward the desert, but Abu kept his eyes on the meerkat, which raced along in the sand behind them. After a few moments, however, the creature's tiny form was lost in the dusty wind.

CHAPTER 4

Jasmine and Aladdin clutched the edges of Magic Carpet tightly and pulled their hoods down over their eyes to keep out the sand. Their two bags sat between them. Abu had moved to Aladdin's feet, where he could wrap the bottom of Aladdin's cloak around him.

The ride was bumpy as Magic Carpet struggled to navigate through the sandstorm. He flipped and flopped, his front edge curling up from the force of the wind.

Jasmine felt one of Magic Carpet's tassels tap her arm to get her attention. She peered out and Carpet pointed ahead, where Jasmine spotted several hazy figures.

A fierce wind suddenly blew under the carpet, causing him to soar straight up for a moment and then spin upside down. Jasmine and Aladdin cried out, but they held tight to Magic Carpet as they were flown head over heels before crash-landing onto the sand.

"Is everyone all right?" asked Jasmine. She had fallen onto her side, but Magic Carpet and the sand cushioned the blow.

"I'm fine," said Aladdin as he helped a dazed Abu out from under one of the bags, which had landed on top of him. Magic Carpet nodded his front tassels to indicate he too was unharmed.

The figures that Jasmine had seen in the distance hurried toward them, revealing a family of nomads leading a trio of camels.

Like Jasmine and Aladdin, the nomads were

protected by heavy hooded cloaks, and the camels wore leather headpieces with stiff flaps on the sides that kept the sand from their eyes.

"We saw you crash," said one of the nomads. "Are you—" She stopped, recognizing Jasmine. "Your Highness! What are you doing out here in the desert?"

Jasmine wasn't sure how much to tell the nomads. Did they know about the myth of the sapphire? Would they even believe it?

The winds were slightly calmer at ground level, making it easier to converse. "I wonder if you've noticed the four-pointed star in the sky?" Jasmine asked the family. "With the blue glow?"

"Yes, of course," said the huskier of the two adult male nomads. "Its light helped us navigate through the wind."

"My great-grandmother believes it's pointing to part of a giant sapphire, woven from stardust by the Sand God," said the youngest nomad, a boy of about twelve. He gestured to the older hunched woman next to him, whose staff was almost twice as tall as she was.

"You know the story?" asked Jasmine. She exchanged a surprised glance with Aladdin.

"Of course!" said the older woman. "But my family does not believe me."

"This is my grandmother, Mariam," said one of the nomads, referring to the older woman. "I am Ahmed." He nodded to the other, younger woman and to the boy. "And this is my wife, Sarah, and our son, Malik. Back there, with the camels, is my brother Omar." He waved toward a thin man who stood behind the others. "We're on our way to stay at the home of my wife's brother in Fahriza until the storms pass."

"Please. Tell us what you know of the legend," said Jasmine.

"*Is* it a legend?" asked Mariam, waving her staff at the churning desert sands. "These winds say otherwise. As does the star-shaped glow in the sky. That light is a signal. The story says a beacon will lead to each of the four missing pieces of the sapphire. Once the pieces are gathered, it will reverse the curse put upon the land by the evil gulin."

A beacon had not been mentioned in the legend Aladdin had found, but Jasmine knew from her reading of fairy tales that there could be many versions of the same story. And clearly, the beacon, like the winds and the falling rainbow star, was not myth but reality. This new bit of information proved that Jasmine's instinct to come to the desert had been a good one, and she felt a momentary boost of confidence.

"That's why we're here," Jasmine told the nomads. "To find the pieces." As she spoke, her words were swallowed up by a gust of wind.

"This way!" Ahmed waved to Aladdin and Jasmine, shouting through the storm.

Aladdin and Jasmine hurried behind Ahmed and the other nomads while Magic Carpet floated behind, carrying Abu and the bags.

"It wasn't actually a gulin who destroyed the

sapphire," said a nearby voice. Jasmine turned to find another nomad next to her, rushing to keep up. At first, she thought it was Omar, Ahmed's brother, but she could see the silhouette of Omar leading the camels through the sandy winds ahead. The nomad next to her was shorter and younger, and his cloak had an unusual green hue to it.

"Well, not a gulin alone," continued the young nomad. "It was a gulin and a human together—and it was an accident."

"A gulin *and* a human?" said Aladdin, his voice filled with doubt.

"Is this a different version of the legend?" asked Jasmine.

The young nomad shook his head. "It's the truth," he replied. "The gulin aren't evil. They're just pranksters. Years and years ago, humans and gulin were friends. But after the sapphire broke, the gulin were forced to go into hiding. That left humans to make up all sorts of stories about them, turning them into monsters, when all they want—I mean *wanted*—was to belong."

"Up ahead!" Ahmed called out. He gestured in front of him and the others followed. The winds grew calmer, and within minutes they were standing in the serene eye of the sandstorm. The eye extended around them in a large circle, more than big enough for all of them, including the camels.

Jasmine could still hear the faint rumble of the winds beyond the eye, and her ears rang in the relative silence. The sun had nearly set, but twilight cast a soft blue glow around them, giving them enough light to see by. A tiny green gecko skittered across the sand past Jasmine's feet. She glanced around for the nomad in the green cloak, to ask him more about the gulin, but he seemed to have vanished. She then noticed a faint shadow in the sand, cast down from above. She glanced up. "Look!" she called out. The blue light illuminating the eye was coming not from the setting sun, but from . . .

"The beacon!" cried Aladdin. Indeed, high in the sky above them, glowing brightly, was the blue star they had seen from the palace.

"The pieces must be here somewhere—or one of them, at least," said Jasmine. If Mariam's story was right, each of the four pieces had its own beacon, which meant only one of them was here in the desert. Still, finding one of the pieces would be a start. "We should dig and see what we find—"

The ground began to vibrate, interrupting her. "What's happening?" asked Sarah. The others looked around worriedly.

Jasmine spotted a hole opening up in the middle of the desert, which quickly grew larger. "Move back!" she shouted to the group as the pit grew wider and wider, pulling in the sand around it. Magic Carpet unfurled, offering a safe haven, but the hole seemed to emit a magnetic force that drew even Carpet toward it. The gap continued to expand, threatening to swallow them all....

CHAPTER
5

Jasmine and the others hurriedly backed away as the sand continued to cascade downward in a fierce spiral. Suddenly, a figure rose up from under the ground: a plump woman, dressed in an outfit that seemed to be made of dozens of scarves, in various shades of yellow and brown. She was seated at a low stone table, and on the table was a backgammon board.

The woman shook her head, tossing sand from her saffron-colored headscarf, and then brushed the last few grains from her lap. Her gold hoop earrings sparkled and her brass bracelets jangled. "Whew!" she declared, after taking in a deep breath. "It's nice to breathe fresh air again! A thousand years stuck under the sand is a thousand years too many, if you ask me!"

Jasmine stared at the woman, baffled. Where had she come from? Why was she seated at a backgammon board? What did she have to do with the shattered sapphire?

"I sense you have some questions?" said the woman, as if reading Jasmine's mind, or at least reading the expression on her face. "Why don't I begin by introducing myself: my name is Ramlah, and I am one of the guardians!"

"Guardians of what?" asked Jasmine.

"Well, of the sapphire shards, of course! And that's all I'll say until you've proven yourself worthy." Ramlah gestured to the backgammon board.

"You want to play a game of backgammon?

Right here? Right now?" asked Jasmine, mystified.

"Well, this board isn't here for decoration!" said Ramlah with a chuckle. "Sit down! Sit down! I haven't got another millennium to wait around—and neither do you."

"This is crazy," Aladdin whispered to Jasmine. "We don't have time for this. We should be digging for the piece."

"I think this is how we get it," Jasmine whispered back. "Look." She nodded to the backgammon board, which had a bluish tint. Instead of the traditional round black and white playing pieces, these were shaped like stars, one set a darker blue than the other. The two dice were the same six-sided cubes Jasmine was familiar with, but in place of the dots on the sides of each die, there were tiny stars.

"I have to play," Jasmine insisted to Aladdin. This guardian was obviously another part of the legend, as was the game. "It's a test of some sort." Jasmine looked to Ramlah for confirmation.

Ramlah winked in reply. "I'll let you roll first," she said, handing Jasmine the dice. "All the rules are the same, but we're only going to play one game. Clear all your pieces off the board and you win!"

Jasmine sat down and rolled a three. Not a great beginning. But backgammon was a game she knew well and was very good at, thanks to years of playing with her father.

Aladdin and the nomads gathered around as the game proceeded. Magic Carpet rose up vertically onto two tassels next to Malik to watch.

Abu hopped onto Aladdin's shoulder for a better view and noticed the tiny gecko that had crossed by earlier was now perched atop the nomads' luggage on one of the camels. The little reptile seemed to be watching the game.

Aladdin wished he'd paid more attention when Jasmine was trying to teach him backgammon so he would know if she was winning. Yet, as the game went on, he could tell from her energetic posture and the brightness in her eyes that she was doing well.

Jasmine allowed herself a small smile. She had succeeded in thinking ahead, strategizing the best way to use her rolls and move her pieces quickly across the board. In a few more turns she would win!

When Ramlah's next turn came, she picked up the dice and dropped them, but instead of landing, they seemed to hover in the air, as if by magic, before finally falling and landing. "Twelve! Lovely!" chirped Ramlah, the hint of a sly smile appearing at the corner of her lips.

Jasmine's smile faded. Was the woman…cheating? Using magic to roll the highest number *and* to roll doubles, which meant she'd be able to play the number twice? This was something Jasmine had never faced with her father. How could she strategize if the guardian was able to control the dice?

Ramlah completed her turn and succeeded

in getting several of her star pieces off the board. "Your roll!" she said cheerfully, handing Jasmine the dice.

Jasmine grasped the dice and hesitated. Would Ramlah let them fall naturally—or use her magic to ensure that Jasmine fell further behind?

"We can stop!" said Ramlah, as if again reading Jasmine's thoughts. "No harm, no foul—but no sapphire!"

Jasmine shook off her worries. She couldn't win if she didn't try. She raised her arm to roll.

"But," added Ramlah, halting Jasmine, "if your next roll costs you the game, you will return with me beneath the sand. I can survive there, but you cannot."

The nomads gasped. "What?" cried Aladdin. "You didn't say anything about that at the start!"

"You're right," admitted Ramlah. "I apologize. A thousand years underground will affect your memory." She tapped her temple, her bangles clinking together.

"This was all a trick," Aladdin said to Jasmine. "Forget it. It's not worth it." Magic Carpet and Abu nodded vigorously in agreement with Aladdin.

Uncertainty and nervousness caused Jasmine's heart to speed up. Was Ramlah serious about dragging Jasmine beneath the sand if she lost? Jasmine glanced at the guardian's face, which had dropped its cheerful smile and now wore a somber, ominous expression.

Jasmine took a deep breath and tried to think clearly. The sapphire shard *was* here. She felt its energy in the sand beneath her feet, which had increased as the game went on. To stop playing meant giving up on retrieving it. If Jasmine and Aladdin turned back now, they would have lost more than a game.

Jasmine inhaled another calming breath and then spoke. "I'll keep playing," she said.

"Roll the dice," said Ramlah, her words less a request than a command.

Jasmine's hand shook as she raised her

arm and threw the two cubes. As they fell, the moment of composure she'd just experienced vanished. Her stomach clenched with terror, as if she had jumped off a cliff. Had she made the wrong decision? What kind of future leader was she that she was filled with so many doubts and fears?

She closed her eyes and heard the dice *clack-clack* onto the table, followed by a loud gasp from Aladdin and the others. Jasmine shut her eyes tight and held her breath. It didn't feel like she was sinking into the earth. She opened one eye and peered down at the dice.

"Well done!" exclaimed Ramlah, her voice bright once again.

Jasmine opened both eyes to find that all the star pieces had risen up from the board. They spun and shimmered a moment before dissolving along with the board, as if it had all been a mirage. "Where—"

"Congratulations, my dear," said Ramlah.

"You've passed the test. You were willing to risk your life to find the sapphire, proving it will be in good hands with you."

A panel slid open in the top of the stone table where the backgammon board had sat, and a marble box rose up. There were flecks of blue in the marble, which twinkled and glowed. The nomads backed away, wary, but Magic Carpet and Aladdin moved closer, intrigued. Abu bounced on Aladdin's shoulder, equally excited.

"Go on," Ramlah told Jasmine. "Open it." There were two brass latches on the front of the box. Jasmine easily lifted one, but the other refused to budge.

"It might be rusty," said Ramlah. "Remember, it's been closed for a long time."

"Maybe it just needs to be jiggled a little," said a familiar voice. The green-cloaked nomad stepped out from behind the camels. The other nomads exchanged questioning looks as he approached the table.

"Excuse me, young man," said Ahmed. "Do we know you?"

"Oh, um . . . no," replied the nomad. "I'm sort of out on my own. Got separated from my group back there." He waved vaguely out beyond the eye before reaching down to lift the second latch, which flipped up easily. Together, he and Jasmine raised the top of the box.

A bright, shimmering blue diamond-shaped shard about a foot long burst out from inside, illuminating the area around the group with an almost blinding brightness.

"The sapphire!" shouted Aladdin as the piece fell to the ground and bounced around erratically, as if propelled by a fidgety energy.

"Oh my!" exclaimed Ramlah. "I guess it's a little agitated from being cooped up for so long."

Jasmine, Aladdin, and the nomads all reached for the shard, but it leapt away, evading their grasp. Abu dived after it and succeeded only in landing flat on his face in the sand. Finally, Magic Carpet rose up and threw himself over the piece.

Light sizzled throughout Carpet's colorful weave, causing every thread to flash and flicker. Sparks burst from his tassels, which snapped and hissed and began to unravel. During the excitement, the green-cloaked nomad darted away, disappearing behind the camels.

After a few moments, Magic Carpet's glowing threads dimmed, and the tapestry lay motionless. A small mound rose in the middle where the shard rested, inert.

"Here." Mariam handed Jasmine a large leather drawstring sack. Aladdin carefully lifted a corner of Magic Carpet, and he and Jasmine scooped the piece into the sack. Jasmine pulled the cords tight.

"Thanks, friend," Aladdin told Magic Carpet, but there was no response.

"Carpet? Are you all right?" asked Jasmine.

Magic Carpet lifted his front tassels and gave a weak nod. He tried to rise off the ground, but after a struggle, he gave up and flopped back down onto the sand.

"Hmm," mused Ramlah. "The sapphire shard must have absorbed your carpet's magic. After so many centuries locked up and separated from the other pieces of the sapphire, it must have built up too much energy—which needed to be counter-acted by your friend's magic in order to stabilize."

"Will Carpet's magic return?" asked Jasmine.

"I really couldn't say," replied Ramlah. "I may have many fantastical talents, but I'm not psychic!" She laughed.

Jasmine watched, pained, as Magic Carpet's front end curled sadly upon hearing this. She glanced at Aladdin and could tell he was equally horrified by the possibility that Magic Carpet's brave action might have cost him his precious enchantment—maybe forever. They each laid a comforting hand on one of his corners, and Abu softly patted one of his now straggly tassels.

"It will be okay," Jasmine told Carpet. "I'm sure that once we find the remaining pieces, you'll be back to normal." Carpet fluttered the corner under Jasmine's hand as if to say, *Don't worry about me.*

"Look!" exclaimed Malik, pointing above them. The others tilted their heads toward the sky.

"The beacon! It's gone!" said Jasmine. Indeed, the sky above them was completely clear. The blue star had vanished. The storm around them still raged, but in the calm eye, they could see the faint gray glow of the coming dawn.

"You no longer need it," explained Ramlah. "Now that you have the piece."

"Finding the piece didn't stop the winds, though," said Jasmine, disappointed.

"They won't stop until all four pieces are found," explained Ramlah.

A puff of cool air blew out of the sack, and it appeared to be trying to tug free of Jasmine's grasp, but she gripped it more firmly. "Why is it doing that if it's stable?" she asked.

"Each piece of the sapphire holds an atmospheric energy," said Ramlah. "This one is related to the winds. It's perfectly normal. Like the winds, it will calm once the sapphire is made whole again. That energy will also protect you, creating a buffer from the winds so that you can pass safely through the sandstorm."

"But how will we find the other pieces?" asked Jasmine.

"Oh yes!" said Ramlah. "I almost forgot that part! The pieces want to be reunited." Ramlah waved at the sack, which continued to tug on Jasmine's hands. "This one will pull you toward the next shard. In addition, each piece will have its own beacon—and its own guardian to protect it and make sure whoever retrieves it can be counted on to restore the sapphire."

Ramlah clapped, her bracelets once again jangling, and the stone table sank back into the sand, vanishing within seconds.

"That's it, I think!" she said. She stretched her arms over her head and smiled at the coming sunrise. "I can't *wait* to catch up on all the news from the last thousand years! Oh! One more thing!" She returned her gaze to Jasmine. "Since a human and a gulin were responsible for shattering the sapphire, a human and a gulin must be present to unlock each shard from its hiding place."

"That can't be true," said Jasmine. "There are no gulin here."

Ramlah frowned. "Hmm." She tapped a ringed finger against her lips. "Did I have that wrong? No . . . I'm pretty sure. . . . Oh, well! A little mystery always makes it more fun, don't you think?"

Jasmine and Aladdin exchanged a stunned look. *"Fun?"* asked Aladdin. "This is life or death."

"I'm sure you're more than up to the challenge," said Ramlah. She waved her arms and her many scarves fluttered, wrapping around her.

"Wait!" Jasmine still had so many questions. "How do we know how far away the other pieces are?"

"Another mystery!" said Ramlah brightly as

she was swallowed up by a swirl of browns and yellows and twinkling golds. Within moments, she had vanished.

Ahmed and his family stared in shock, all of them overwhelmed by what they had witnessed. "That was quite . . ."

"Incredible!" exclaimed Malik.

The sack tugged harder, as if trying to get Jasmine's attention. "It's pulling us south . . . I think," she said. Since Ahmed's family was going in that direction, they offered to accompany Jasmine and Aladdin, who gratefully accepted.

While Malik helped Aladdin roll up Carpet, Jasmine looked around for the green-cloaked nomad. He had been right in his claim that a human and a gulin had shattered the sapphire, and she wanted to ask him more about his version of the legend—but there was no sign of him.

"Where did that young man go?" asked Sarah, echoing Jasmine's thoughts.

Abu pointed toward the camels. *"Chir, chir, chir,*

CHIR!" he exclaimed, holding up four fingers.

The others looked at the camels. "Where did that camel come from?" asked Ahmed—for there were now four. Jasmine noticed one was slightly smaller than the others and seemed to have a faint green tinge to its fur.

"Maybe it belongs to that other nomad," suggested Aladdin.

Ahmed stepped toward the camel, but the small creature bolted, dashing out of the eye and disappearing into the storm.

In the desert, the camel shape-shifted into a lizard, the clear scales over its eyes protecting its vision from the blowing sand. It raced back toward Agrabah, shifting once again into a snake as it neared a small opening in the sand just outside of the city. It slithered into the hole, and with one last flick of its tail, it vanished beneath the surface.

CHAPTER 6

Below Agrabah, an intricate series of narrow tunnels led to a large, cavernous meeting place. There, the gulin leader, Umab, had summoned the entire gulin population, numbering a hundred or so, for an announcement. "The winds outside have grown worse and they show no sign of letting up," said Umab. "So far, the tunnels have not been affected, but it is more imperative than ever that everyone remain far away from any passages that lead to the surface...."

Most of the gulin gathered in the cavern were in their wraithlike gulin form and hovered above the floor listlessly. Although they resembled humans in their shape, their bodies had a greenish hue and were nearly transparent. Legs allowed them to walk, but they could also move by floating. A few of the gulin in the room lazily shape-shifted from one small creature to the next, transforming from mouse to crab to guinea fowl to tortoise, bored by Umab's speech and eager to return to their individual caves and go back to sleep.

The cavern was decorated with samples of the shiny objects that all gulin loved, from brass decanters to copper medallions. Each item sat on its own shelf carved into the red clay walls. Reflections of some items could be seen in the pool of water at the bottom of a grotto near the back of the cavern.

Layli, one of the smaller gulin, stood near the grotto, paying only faint attention to Umab. Her focus was on the different cavern entrances as she searched for some sign of her brother. Where was he?

She felt something squeeze her ankle and looked down to see that a snake had wrapped itself around her foot. She frowned and kicked it off. "Where have you *been*?" she whispered to the snake—even though she had already guessed the answer.

The snake flopped onto the dirt floor and shape-shifted into a flying beetle. It flew up to Layli's face, flicking its green wings at her nose.

She batted it away. "Bedair! Stop it!" she hissed.

"Layli? Is there a problem?" Umab called from her stone podium. A few gulin cast mildly curious glances to the back of the cavern.

"No, Umab. I'm sorry."

"As I was *saying*," continued Umab. "The tunnels should be used only to get from one cave to the next. There should be no wandering...."

The beetle shape-shifted once more, transforming into Layli's gulin brother, Bedair.

"I saw it, Layli," said Bedair.

"*Shhh.*"

Bedair lowered his voice. "I saw a piece of the sapphire!"

"If Umab finds out you were aboveground again—"

"You're not listening to me—"

"I am," said Layli. "And I *told* you—I'm tired of hearing this story." Bedair had been talking about the sapphire for decades—*centuries*! As he told it, Bedair and Niddal, his human best friend, had been competing in one of their challenges, this one a race to the top of the arch over the entrance gates to the city to see who could touch the sapphire first. Bedair had shape-shifted into a human boy to make it a fair contest. Niddal had won, but his shirt had gotten snagged on one of the iron prongs holding the giant gem in place. Bedair had transformed into a bear in order to have the strength to pull Niddal free, but the sapphire had come loose and fallen....

There were so many unbelievable parts of this story, but the most ridiculous was the idea that a human and a gulin could be best friends! Everyone knew humans feared the gulin, which was why the gulin stayed in their homes underground.

"It's *not* a story," Bedair said now. "And I can prove it. They have the first piece and they're out looking for the rest, but we have to help them!"

"They who?" said Layli. "What are you talking about?"

"Layli! Bedair!" Umab called out from the front of the cavern. "If what you have to say is so important, why don't you share it with the rest of us?"

Bedair responded by floating forward, toward Umab.

"No, Bedair . . . ," protested Layli, but Bedair ignored her.

"These winds have come because the one thousand years is up!" declared Bedair. The news he had to share was too important to keep quiet.

"We need to reunite the pieces of the sapphire before it's too late!"

"Not this sapphire nonsense again," mumbled a nearby gulin. More moans and grumbles accompanied this comment.

"The first piece has been found! In the desert!" continued Bedair. "I saw it! I helped Princess Jasmine retrieve it!"

Umab scowled. "You helped Princess Jasmine, Bedair? The current Sultan of Agrabah's daughter? *Really?*"

"I'm not making it up! I overheard her and her friend Aladdin talking about searching for the pieces, and I followed them out to the desert, and—"

"*Followed?*" exclaimed Umab. "Please tell me you didn't try to speak to them." Gulin were strictly forbidden to interact with humans.

"Don't worry," replied Bedair. "I shape-shifted into a nomad and then into a camel when they noticed me."

"*They noticed you?*" Umab's large dark-green eyes went wide in horror. Murmurs rippled through the gulin crowd.

Layli groaned. Her brother had admitted to breaking almost every gulin rule. Not only had he ventured to the surface, but he had shape-shifted *in front of* humans.

The other gulin moved aside as Umab floated off her podium and made her way toward Bedair. "Bedair, I have warned you over and over—if humans once again believe in us, there is no end to what they will blame us for. They could blame us for these sandstorms!" The walls rumbled as if to echo Umab's words. An emerald ring tumbled from its ledge to the cavern floor. Umab scooped up the fallen ring and continued toward Bedair.

"But if we restore the sapphire, the winds will stop," protested Bedair. "We'll have helped the humans, and they'll see that their stories about us aren't true. We'll be able to go above again when-ever we want!"

"Who wants to go above?" snarled a gulin. The others mumbled in agreement. Most of them had lost their listlessness and were now glaring at Bedair.

Bedair glanced around at the angry faces, sad that none of them remembered. "We used to have fun in Agrabah!" he said. "Playing pranks? Making humans laugh? You must remember *some* of it." The gulin shook their heads and turned away. Bedair groaned in frustration. Centuries of Umab insisting that gulin interactions with humans had always been negative—and that this is why they had gone underground—had brainwashed the gulin. They may have had doubts initially, but over the years they came to assume their memories were false and that Umab's stories were true. Bedair knew Umab believed she was protecting the gulin, but he was certain the fear her stories had instilled had robbed the gulin, including Layli, of all potential for joy.

"There will be no more of this nonsense," said

Umab as she reached Bedair, her voice dark with warning. "Do you realize the danger you put us in? The humans could flood the tunnels, flush us out—and destroy the only home we have."

All of the gulin were alert now, and they crowded around Bedair. Layli hurriedly made her way through them, to her brother's side.

"He understands, Umab," said Layli quickly. "He'll stay inside. I'll make sure—"

"I can't!" protested Bedair. "I have to go back out. They need us. They need a gulin to—"

"*Enough!*" shouted Umab. Her voice echoed off the walls. "It pains me to do this, Bedair, but you just admitted it yourself—you can't be trusted to stay out of sight of humans."

Before Bedair or Layli could reply, Umab swept one arm in an arc over Bedair's head. The other gulin gasped as Bedair shrunk down into a green wisp, which was absorbed into the emerald of the ring in Umab's other hand.

"No!" cried Layli.

"I'm sorry, Layli, but you can see why this was necessary," said Umab, nodding at the flashing ring. "It's my job to protect all of us. Especially in such turbulent times."

"How long does he have to stay in there?" asked Layli, hoping the punishment would not be more than a day or two.

"Until I decide it's safe for him to be released," replied Umab. "Definitely not before the storms have passed." The emerald in the ring flashed wildly in response to this.

"But—"

"Bedair will be better off in there," said Umab as she handed the ring to Layli. "He will be safe."

CHAPTER 7

Layli sat in the small private cave where she lived with Bedair, the ring resting on a rock. The light inside pulsed sadly. "I'm sorry," said Layli, guessing her brother's thoughts. "You know there's no way I can make Umab change her mind. She's worried. About you, about all of us."

The emerald flashed once, its beam reflecting off a pretty pendant, one of the dozens of shiny objects decorating their cave. Most of the items adorning the tunnels' caverns had decayed or become tarnished over the centuries. Many of those in Layli and Bedair's cave were from Bedair's illicit visits to the surface, however, and they still sparkled and gleamed. For a long time, Layli had hidden these, digging holes in the walls and smoothing the clay over them. But over the decades, the other gulin kept more and more to themselves, sleeping and rarely venturing out from their caves unless summoned to an assembly by Umab.

Bedair insisted the gulin's love of sparkling and gleaming things went deeper than a meaningless attraction. He believed it was an important part of their naturally playful spirit, which was also responsible for their shape-shifting and their good-natured pranking of humans before the gulin disappeared underground.

Although Layli always scoffed when Bedair made these claims, she did sometimes wonder, deep down, if he was right. She refused to admit it to Bedair, but she occasionally *did* have vague

recollections of happy times outside the tunnels —
of adventures, and of interactions with the
people of Agrabah. For the other gulin, any
memories like these had faded as century after
century passed, until they seemed like dreams.
But the other gulin didn't have Bedair and his
colorful tales of life above.

Yet her doubts were always there. Was what
she remembered true? Or was it just the vividness
of Bedair's stories that brought the images to life in
her mind?

The ring remained dark and Layli could picture
Bedair inside, brooding and depressed. These
winds could last for years. How could he possibly
bear being trapped for that long?

And how could *she* bear a life without Bedair
constantly irritating her with his pranks and
pestering her to sneak out with him? She needed,
at least, to be able to communicate with him.

"Remember when we used to shape-shift into
mice and sneak into the lamps in the assembly

room to raise the flames inside higher and lower?" Layli asked the ring. "We used a code to communicate. Do you remember it?" It had been a couple of centuries earlier that they'd stopped the game. Layli had grown bored with it, just as the other gulin had grown bored pranking only each other. This was another reason to believe Bedair's claim that humans had once enjoyed the gulin and their mischievous way. The gulin's joy in life had been fooling their human friends and making them laugh. Laughter was so rare now in the tunnels.

The ring flashed on and off once, followed by a series of slow and fast blinks. Layli racked her memory to decode it. Bedair repeated the pattern, and finally it came back to her. "Yes! I remember!" she said, stating both her own thoughts and what Bedair had just communicated.

The ring continued to flash, sometimes too quickly for Layli to keep up. "Slow down!" she said more than once, but eventually she understood. "No, Bedair. I can't," she told her brother. "What if Umab caught me? We'd both end up locked in rings." The emerald sent out a fierce glow followed by a series of short pulses.

Layli floated around the cave, agitated. "Who cares what happens up there? It doesn't affect us as long as we stay here. We're *safe* here."

There was a pause and then the ring flashed on and off softly, pleadingly. *If you won't do it for Agrabah, do it for me.*

Layli was silent. She loved Bedair. He was the only family she had—or had ever had. Gulin had formed when the earth was created, spun from the same magical dust. Like humans, there were boys and girls, but unlike humans, the gulin had no parents. Instead, when they were formed, they divided off into small groups of siblings. Some gulin had as many as ten brothers and sisters. Others, like Layli and Bedair, had only each other. Although the gulin had no parents, they did have Umab. She watched over all of them like a wise protector, one who was loving yet strict.

"It's too dangerous," insisted Layli. The emerald flashed again and again as Bedair continued to argue and beg, trying to persuade Layli that finding the sapphire would restore the weather and the relations between human and gulin.

Layli remained skeptical of Bedair's claims—but what if he was right about even a part of it? Bedair's frequent forbidden trips to the surface made him more likely to know what was truly going on above than even Umab.

If finding the sapphire led to Umab freeing Bedair, Layli had to try. "I'll do it," she said.

A few minutes later, Layli, now in the form of a viper, peered out of the tiny hole that Bedair had entered earlier. She watched the sand whip past and hesitated, nervous and afraid. A gulin possessed the strengths of whatever form they shape-shifted into, but they were also plagued by the vulnerabilities that came along with their chosen incarnation. A shape-shifted gulin needed food, rest, and shelter. They could be injured or even killed.

A green glow lit up the hole around her, coming from the emerald ring she wore on her tail, as Bedair repeated the instructions he had given her earlier.

She hissed in response. *I know, I know.* She reminded herself that she was doing this for her brother, and that made it worth all the risks. She steeled herself and slithered out of the hole.

Layli was instantly flung by the wind, but she shape-shifted into an elephant and landed with a *thump* on her four sturdy feet. The sand battered her green-tinted leathery skin, but she stood firm. The ring now sat at the tip of one tusk and flashed: *Well done!*

Layli took a breath. The memories she had of being aboveground remained hazy, but there was something about breathing the air outside the tunnels that made her more certain those memories were real.

A dusty wind smacked against her head, causing her giant ears to flap and sending sand up her trunk. She shook her huge head and snorted out the sand. She could feel a dangerous energy coming through the wind and immediately sensed something unnatural about what was happening, something that needed to be fixed.

Her gulin sensibility had been awakened by the magic in the atmosphere, and she felt energized in a way she hadn't in years . . . decades . . . *centuries*. She took a deep breath, reared back on her hind legs, and then galloped into the storm.

CHAPTER 8

High atop Ahmed's lead camel, Jasmine peered ahead through the windblown sand toward seemingly endless dunes. Magic Carpet lay quietly on the back of the camel, behind the saddle. Sarah followed on the second camel, and Mariam was on the third. Ahmed, Malik, and Omar walked alongside, as did Aladdin, with Abu on his shoulder.

Aladdin reached up to pat Carpet. "How are you doing, friend?" he asked. Carpet lifted two tassels, giving Aladdin a weak thumbs-up.

The sack with the sapphire piece swung beside Jasmine, its strings gripped in her left hand. The shard was surprisingly light despite its size— nearly weightless. As the guardian had promised, the piece seemed to cast a protective perimeter around them so that the only wind Jasmine felt was the occasional puff of cool air emitted from the sack as it gently pulled her forward.

They had been traveling for several hours now, and Jasmine's stomach rumbled with hunger. They had stopped once at an oasis to rest the camels and nap briefly, but Jasmine had soon been awakened by worry and by the tugging of the sack's strings, which she had tied around her wrist. The group had shared a small breakfast of dates and bread at the oasis, but it was now nearly noon. Another day was passing and Jasmine's hope that the remaining sapphire pieces would be found in the desert was quickly fading.

The sack let out an impatient puff of air. "I want to find the other shards, too," Jasmine told it.

She kept her eyes on the horizon and saw a hazy image appear in the distance. "I see something!" she shouted.

"The beacon?" asked Aladdin.

"No, it's . . ." Jasmine squinted as the image seemed to divide, forming two figures, then several—another family: a man and a woman, and two small girls riding a goat. A donkey trudged behind them, carrying several bags.

"Cousin!" the man shouted, waving toward Jasmine's group. Sarah waved back and climbed down from her camel to introduce the family as they approached.

"This is my cousin Yusuf," said Sarah. "And his wife, Noor, and their daughters, Mona and Deena. They live in Al-Bandar, a village on the Gulf." Omar helped Mariam down from the camel so she could hug the girls.

"What are you doing out here in the desert?" Ahmed asked Yusuf.

"Things are not good in the Gulf," replied Yusuf.

"For the past week we've had constant rains and deadly whirlpools. Hundreds of dead fish have washed up onto the shores each day."

"Yusuf nearly drowned when his fishing boat capsized," said Noor. They too were on their way to stay with Sarah's brother in Fahriza, until the weather had calmed in the Gulf.

Jasmine and Aladdin exchanged a look. The piece they'd captured had been found in the midst of a sandstorm. It seemed that either the shard's unstable energy had triggered the storm, or the storm had appeared to signal where the shard lay. Whichever was the case, it was possible another piece of the sapphire had landed where these rains and whirlpools were occurring—and was maybe even the cause of them.

"Do you think the second piece might be there?" Aladdin asked Jasmine.

Jasmine nodded. The sack at her side bounced and swung, seemingly in agreement. The family stared at it in alarm.

"Have you trapped an animal in there?" asked Mona.

"Not exactly," replied Jasmine. She filled the family in on the reason for their journey and everything that had happened so far.

"We saw it!" cried Deena. "The blue star in the sky!"

"It's out over the Gulf," said Mona.

Noor nodded. "We had thought it was just a reflection off the surface of the water," she said. "But it now seems that it might be—"

"The beacon!" Jasmine and Aladdin said together.

Yusuf told Jasmine that the fishing village was not far. "Just over the next dune, you can see the outskirts of Al-Bandar," he said.

Jasmine and Aladdin insisted Ahmed and his family continue on with their relatives to Fahriza. "We'll be fine on our own," she assured them. She lifted up the sack containing the sapphire shard. "After all, we have *this* to guide us to the next piece—and protect us."

"Take one of our camels, at least," offered Ahmed. "To carry your carpet and supplies."

Jasmine shook her head. She felt they were already in enough debt to Ahmed and his family.

"I can carry Carpet," Aladdin insisted. He tossed Carpet over his shoulder, and then took a bag in one hand. Jasmine picked up the other.

Abu held out his hands to carry the pouch of dates and nuts. "I don't think so, Abu," said Aladdin. "That pouch would be a lot lighter before we got very far." Abu shrugged innocently. "You can carry this." Aladdin handed the monkey an empty water bag. Abu frowned and snorted. He stomped ahead, dragging the bag behind him.

Jasmine thanked her new friends for all their help before the two groups parted.

"You're doing a great and brave thing, Your Highness," Sarah told Jasmine. "It is a rare royal who would risk all on such a dangerous quest." The rest of her family nodded.

"She's a rare princess," said Aladdin, smiling proudly at Jasmine.

Jasmine smiled in return, but her smile was not as assured. She might be doing a brave thing, and the second piece of the sapphire might lie ahead—but would a better leader have already found all four pieces?

As Aladdin and Jasmine climbed the dune, they noticed bits of scrub brush growing up from the sand, evidence of water nearby.

Aladdin grunted and shifted the carpet to his opposite shoulder. "I guess it's only fair that I carry *you* for a while," he said. "After you've carried me so many places." Carpet patted Aladdin on the back encouragingly.

Neither Aladdin nor Jasmine noticed a small, greenish vole creeping behind them. But Abu did. He chittered in alarm and slapped Aladdin on the ankle with the empty water bottle.

"Quit that," said Aladdin. "We're not stopping for a snack."

Abu hit Aladdin again as the vole raced past them and then circled around. Something green sparkled from one of its paws.

"Does that rat have a ring on its leg?" asked Aladdin.

"That's a vole, not a rat," said Jasmine. She set down her bag and took an almond from a pouch at her waist. "Hello, there, little guy," she called out to the creature. "Would you like a nut?" The emerald in the ring flashed on and off, seemingly in reply.

"Did you see that?" asked Aladdin. "It's like there's a light inside there."

Jasmine stepped closer, but as she did, the vole suddenly transformed into a panther and snatched the sack containing the sapphire shard in its jaws. The panther bit through the string that tied the sack to Jasmine's wrist and dashed away.

CHAPTER 9

Layli ran, her panther legs speeding her across the desert floor. The ring, now wrapped around a claw, pulsed angrily. Bedair was upset with her for stealing the shard, but Layli didn't trust the humans. She'd decided to take the piece back to the tunnels. Once Umab saw it, she'd realize Bedair had been telling the truth. Layli was sure this would persuade Umab to free Bedair from the ring. The gulin leader could then assemble a team of gulin to retrieve the rest of the sapphire.

Layli glanced behind her. The princess was chasing after her. The tall boy had set down the carpet next to the little monkey and was running after her as well. They were no match for her panther speed, but sand got into her eyes and she stumbled. She shape-shifted into a lizard, but the sack with the sapphire shard tugged at her, trying to pull her back toward the princess, and Layli found herself tumbling end over end.

Jasmine and Aladdin raced toward the flashing green light. The panther had somehow disappeared, and the ring seemed to be moving by itself across the sand. As they got closer, Jasmine could see the ring was actually now on the arm of a spotted green lizard, which was fighting to keep hold of the sack in its teeth. The lizard darted in front of Jasmine, who lost her balance as she tried to sidestep the reptile.

The creature then dashed past Aladdin. He sprinted after it, quickly closing in. The sack soon proved too heavy and cumbersome, causing the lizard to drop it, sending it tumbling across the sand toward Jasmine.

The lizard had dropped the ring as well and Aladdin scooped it up. He then watched in amazement as the lizard transformed into a greenish wraithlike girl, who floated up in front of him. "A gulin!" he cried in shock. The emerald in the ring sparkled wildly. Aladdin squinted at it, intrigued. "Is there a genie in here?"

Layli shape-shifted into a crow, plucked the ring from Aladdin's hand, and returned to her gulin form.

"Wow," said Aladdin. "That was amazing!"

Layli had to admit it *felt* amazing. It had been a long time since she'd shifted so many times in one day, much less a matter of minutes.

Jasmine, carrying the sack, darted across the sand and stopped next to Aladdin. Abu had left Carpet and the bags, and he hurried up to join his friends.

Jasmine stared at Layli. "Who . . . ?"

"It's a gulin," said Aladdin. "In the flesh—or rather, in the . . . whatever it is gulin are made of."

Layli glared at Aladdin. "I'm a *she*, not an *it*," she snapped. "I'm Layli. And this is my brother, Bedair." She held up the ring. The emerald flashed once.

Abu widened his eyes at the blinking emerald, while Jasmine and Aladdin exchanged a curious glance. "Nice to, um, meet you," Jasmine said to the ring.

The ring flashed and Layli translated. "You've already met. At the backgammon game." Another series of bright pulses flickered from the ring. "He helped you open the box. Whatever *that* means."

So Ramlah had been right, Jasmine realized. A gulin and human *had* retrieved the piece together. "Why is he in the ring?" Jasmine asked Layli.

"Because of *you*!" cried Layli. The ring glowed darkly. "All right, not because of you *exactly*. It's a long story, but he's stuck and that's why I'm here.

He made me come." Another sharp flash. "To help you," Layli added reluctantly.

"If you're here to help, why did you steal *this*?" asked Jasmine, lifting the sack.

Layli hesitated. *Tell them,* Bedair flashed. Layli sighed and explained about Umab and the gulin rules. "I just want Bedair free. I know humans hate gulin. Why should you help me?"

"Because Aladdin and I need you to help *us*," replied Jasmine.

The ring flashed. "That's what Bedair says," said Layli.

"You can't restore the sapphire alone," continued Jasmine. "And neither can we."

Another flash. "Yes," Layli said with a nod. "Bedair said that, too."

"So?" asked Jasmine. "Can we work together?"

Layli studied Jasmine. The princess seemed sincere, and Layli knew Bedair would not leave her alone until she agreed.

"Yes, all right," Layli said finally.

"Do you really trust her?" Aladdin whispered to Jasmine as they made their way back to Carpet and the bags.

"We have to. Just as she has to trust us," replied Jasmine.

"I don't know," said Aladdin. He cast a skeptical glance back at Layli, who was nodding at something the ring—or rather Bedair—was saying to her.

"Once upon a time, I trusted a thief I met in the streets of Agrabah," said Jasmine. "Because I knew he was a good person underneath. And I was not proved wrong." She gave Aladdin a sly smile.

"Well, that's . . . I—I guess . . . ," stuttered Aladdin. "All right, all right. I get your point."

Layli floated up toward them. "Are you talking about me?" she demanded.

"Only to say that we're glad you found us," replied Jasmine.

They had reached the bags. Aladdin glanced down at Carpet, not eager to have to haul the heavy tapestry the rest of the way up the hill. "I don't suppose you'd like to shape-shift into a camel and carry these things for us?" he asked Layli.

Layli glared at him. "I'm not your pack animal," she snapped.

"I didn't mean—it's just, it would make it easier and faster—and that's what we all want, right?" asked Aladdin. Abu chittered in agreement.

Layli responded by shape-shifting into a flea. She buzzed past Aladdin's face and then circled Abu's head. The monkey batted at her in vain.

"I guess she told *you*," Jasmine said with a laugh.

As Yusuf had promised, the village was visible once they reached the top of the dune. With the sapphire shard leading the way, they passed more and more greenery as they got closer to the Gulf:

tiny date palms and small orchards of trees bearing figs and apricots, almonds and pistachios. Abu scurried beneath the trees, gathering up any fallen fruit.

Stone and clay houses appeared as well, beneath a dark gray sky. The gray shifted and churned, as if alive.

Jasmine felt a *plink* of cool water on her cheek.

"Rain," said Aladdin, holding out his palm.

"Just a sprinkle," replied Jasmine, but as they continued on, the rain grew heavier. Aladdin and Jasmine pulled up their hoods, but Jasmine knew their cloaks would not keep out the rain for long.

Layli shape-shifted into a goose and waddled next to the others. The rain dropped off her waterproof feathers, which she occasionally fluttered, dousing Abu, who shrieked in protest.

"It's stopped moving," said Aladdin, nodding to the sack in Jasmine's hand.

Jasmine had noticed this as well. The pull had lessened as they neared the Gulf. "It must be because we've come to the right place." She said this with as much assurance as possible—even though she *wasn't* sure.

Jasmine searched through the downpour for the beacon, but all she could see in the cloudy sky ahead was gray and more gray.

At last they reached the village. Small stone homes lined a narrow street, which opened onto a large town square. Layli shape-shifted into a human: a small girl with dark hair, looking as if she could be Jasmine's green-cloaked younger sister. A few villagers blinked in surprise.

"You might want to limit the shape-shifting thing in public," Aladdin whispered to Layli.

"Difficult to see anything in the rain, isn't it?" Layli replied loudly. Hearing this, the confused villagers brushed raindrops from their eyes, shrugged, and moved on.

Jasmine smiled. She pointed toward the far side of the square, where there was a market underneath a cover of wide tarps. "We might be able to get more information there about the rains," she said.

Aladdin heaved Magic Carpet off his shoulders. "We need to find a place to store Carpet first." The rain had soaked through the tapestry's wool fibers, making it twice as heavy.

"Over there," said Jasmine. She led the group to stables next to the market, where the vendors' donkeys and camels had been housed. They rented a small stall for Carpet. "We'll be back as soon as we can," Jasmine told Carpet as Aladdin unrolled their wet friend onto the straw to dry out. Carpet waved his tassels, assuring Aladdin and Jasmine that he would be fine.

As they exited the stables, they heard a distinctive loud voice rise above the hum of the crowd inside the market.

"I'll give you two for five . . . or I could take ten for three—return customer discount. . . . No, no—I'm not paying over eleven. And that's my absolute, final offer."

Jasmine and Aladdin exchanged a look and searched the crowd. They caught a glimpse of a blue cheek, a sliver of a black ponytail, and the curve of a large gold hoop in a big blue ear.

"Could it be ...?" Jasmine asked Aladdin.

Aladdin nodded and grinned. He cupped his hands around his mouth and shouted: "Genie!"

CHAPTER
10

"**Al**!" A blue arm rose above the crowd and waved. Aladdin and Jasmine weaved their way under the tarps, followed by Abu and Layli. Each of the dozen or so food stalls was surrounded by several people, but it wasn't hard to keep the tall—and blue—Genie in sight. They found him in front of a fruit cart, a dozen pomegranates cradled in one arm. Genie dropped his purchases into a basket at his feet and grabbed Aladdin, pulling him into a crushing hug.

"*Can't ... breathe ...*," Aladdin choked out.

Genie released Aladdin. "Me too, me too. Totally taking my breath away to see you both!" He beamed a warm smile at Jasmine. "My friends! My champions. What fun we had—aside from that pesky Jafar. What good times!" Genie wiped a happy tear from his eyes. "But enough reminiscing. Have a pom!" He tossed pomegranates to Aladdin and Jasmine.

"This is our friend Layli." Jasmine gestured to Layli, standing shyly off to the side.

"Hello!" said Genie. "Any friend of Aladdin and Jasmine—et cetera, et cetera!" He tossed Layli a pomegranate as well.

"Excuse me. You have not paid for those," scolded the fruit seller, a squat elderly woman wearing a shawl embroidered with colorful fruits.

"I believe we said seven?" replied Genie, making a show of searching through a tiny silk bag.

"We did *not*," replied the woman. "You owe me at least twice that."

"Seven and a half."

Aladdin leaned over to Genie and whispered. "Why do you need to bargain? Can't you just wish for whatever you want?"

"Where's the fun in that?" replied Genie. He flicked his thumb against his index finger, as if flipping an invisible coin. A moment later, a large gold disk appeared in the air over the woman's head. It hung there a moment before dropping into her hand. "There you go," said Genie. "Worth ten times what you asked, at least. Keep the change."

"You wear me out, my friend," said the fruit-seller as she pocketed the coin.

"Oh, you love it," replied Genie with a wink. He snapped his fingers and produced a bouquet of wildflowers. He handed them to the fruit seller and her frown instantly softened into a smile.

Layli was still staring at her pomegranate, unsure what to do with it. Abu, annoyed he hadn't been given one of his own, jumped onto Layli's arm and snatched hers. "Hey!" she protested. Abu ignored her and darted behind a barrel of grains to enjoy the fruit in peace.

"Here," said Jasmine. She held out a handful of the fruit's ruby seeds to Layli.

Following Aladdin and Jasmine's lead, Layli popped the seeds into her mouth and chewed. Her eyes went wide. The seeds were juicy—sweet and sour at the same time. Eating was something Layli had not done since the gulin had gone underground. Along with her memories of shape-shifting, her memories of the tastes and smells of food had faded over the centuries.

Genie noticed the ring on Layli's finger flashing. "Is that what I think it is?" he asked. Having been trapped in a lamp for ten thousand years made Genie acutely sensitive to the possibility of his magic brethren being similarly imprisoned.

"No," said Layli as she hid her arm behind her back. "It's just catching the sunlight. That's all."

"There *is* no sunlight," Genie pointed out. He studied Layli's green cloak and the faint green tinge to her skin. "If I'm not mistaken," he said. "You're a gulin!"

"You know about the gulin?" asked Aladdin.

"Do *I* know about the gulin?" Genie snorted out an amazed laugh. "We're second cousins! Or is it third cousins once removed? Or, wait, maybe it's first cousins of the third cousins of my aunt on my mother's side. Anyway—we're family!"

Genie leaned around Layli and called to the ring. "Come on out! Join the party!"

Layli pulled her hand protectively to her chest. "He can't come out. He's trapped."

"I didn't think gulin had masters," said Genie.

"We don't!" replied Layli, insulted by the idea. "We're completely independent. It was a gulin who trapped him. Our leader, Umab."

Jasmine filled Genie in on everything that had happened since they left Agrabah: the sandstorms and their discovery of the curse. She showed him the sack with the first shard, told him about the backgammon game, and explained how it had absorbed Carpet's magic.

"No! Say it ain't so!" exclaimed Genie at this last piece of news. "Poor M.C." He shook his head. "That's gotta be hard on a rug."

Bedair flashed from inside the ring, adding his own details to the story. Layli was surprised Genie understood, but also dismayed. She'd thought the code was private, just for her and Bedair.

"Oh, that code goes *waaaaay* back," explained Genie. "It's a way to communicate when you're stuck in a lamp—or a ring. Or when you don't want humans to know what you're talking about." He glanced apologetically at Aladdin and Jasmine. "No offense."

Genie confirmed that the rains had arrived in Al-Bandar shortly after the appearance of the falling rainbow star. At first, everyone had assumed it was just a brief storm that would quickly pass. But as the days went on, the rains grew worse and more unpredictable. There would be a brief let up, followed by a sudden downpour. The fishermen reported being caught in strange currents, and soon hundreds of fish began washing up dead on the sand.

As Genie talked, he led the group through the village toward the shore. Jasmine and Aladdin hurried to keep pace with Genie, pulling up their hoods to keep out the rain. Abu picked up a small palm frond from the road and held it over his head. Layli shape-shifted into a pelican and flew above the others, the emerald ring now circling one leg.

There was a slight hill leading to the shore. The air had a musty, salty smell Jasmine had noticed in the marketplace, but which now hit her full force. When they reached the top of the hill, the Gulf came into view, a wide blue expanse, with foamy crests of white caused by the choppy waves. Jasmine was in awe.

Although Aladdin had taken Jasmine over oceans on their first trip aboard Magic Carpet, Jasmine had never seen such a large body of water up close. But *this* ... it was magnificent and seemed to go on forever.

Layli, too, was stunned. She had never seen anything this big and wondrous. It was just water, but it seemed like a living thing—an angry, roaring one—sending out a *whoosh* and a *crash* as each wave smashed onto the sand.

In one day, Layli had seen more of the world than she had seen in millennia! The earth suddenly felt precious to her, and finding the sapphire pieces became urgent. She *had* to prevent all this wonder from being destroyed!

Layli flew ahead and noticed that the beach was speckled with oblong silver shells. Suddenly, some of the shells moved. They weren't shells— they were fish! They flailed helplessly on the sand, washed up by the erratic tide.

"*Caw! Caw!*" she called, and swooped down to snatch up one of the fish and toss it back into the Gulf.

Jasmine and Aladdin joined her, but it was

difficult to keep hold of the slippery, squirming fish. Jasmine knew they were wasting time. They needed to find the sapphire piece to save the fish that were still out in the Gulf and not yet washed ashore.

A *squawk* above snapped Jasmine out of her daze. Layli circled overhead, the emerald around her leg blinking on and off. She waved a wing out over the water. Jasmine searched the gray waves and gray skies. Layli squawked again and flew farther out. The green-feathered pelican was lost for a moment in the clouds, but it emerged as the clouds parted, revealing a bright blue light, shaped like a star.

"The beacon!" shouted Jasmine.

CHAPTER
11

Another cloud passed in front of the shape, but the beacon's blue glow was still visible, and Jasmine could see what seemed to be its reflection: a blue star-shaped shimmer on the surface of a wave as it crested upward. "We need to get a boat," she told the others. They hurried to a nearby dock, where a few fishermen were struggling with the ropes to their boats, which had been pulled loose from their poles by the waves. None of the fishermen would agree to take the group out, no matter how much money Jasmine offered.

"Too dangerous," they all answered. Nor would any agree to let Jasmine rent their boats. "These tides have smashed and sank more than a dozen boats already," insisted one of the men.

"If we can't take someone else's boat, we'll have to take our own," said Genie. Moments later, he had conjured up a gleaming white skiff.

The group headed out, navigating as best they could while Layli flew above them. Jasmine had never sailed a boat, nor had Aladdin. Jasmine held tight to the sack with the sapphire piece, which seemed to have come alive again, urging them onward. The boat had a small sail, but it was soon ripped from the mast and blown out to sea. Genie and Aladdin wrestled with the rudder as they tried to steer toward the beacon. Genie wished them each an oar, but although they rowed as hard as they could, it did little good against the fierce current. Periodically, they would pass a whirlpool, which would spin the boat around and send it off course.

Seawater splashed into their eyes. Abu gripped the side of the boat, his little face taking on the same green tinge as Layli's feathers as she flapped fiercely, fighting the wind above the boat.

"We can't get close enough!" shouted Jasmine as they were caught in another whirlpool.

Layli flew ahead, and when she reached the location of the beacon, she entered a tiny pocket of calm. She glanced back at the boat. Jasmine had joined Aladdin and Genie at the rudder, and the three were struggling to keep the boat from spinning.

Green flashes blinked from the ring on Layli's leg: Bedair, telling her what she needed to do. Layli nodded and dove toward the beacon's reflection in the waves. She shape-shifted into a carp as she hit the surface and plunged down.

The ring was now wrapped around her fish tail. Although the water was calm in this spot, sand swirled about, kicked up by the current outside the pocket, making it difficult to see. But Layli could feel the magical energy from the piece. It was definitely close. Her gulin sensibility guided her downward, and she slammed into something hard. She blinked her wide carp eyes, dazed, and heard a strange watery singing coming from somewhere nearby. A moment later, she felt herself being propelled upward.

Layli was thrown out of the water and into the skiff, which had finally reached the pocket. Layli flopped around a moment, still shaking off her daze, and then shape-shifted into her human form.

"Did you find anything?" asked Jasmine.

"I don't know," replied Layli. "I hit something, but it started to move, and then—"

"Look!" Aladdin pointed at three iridescent catfish that had appeared in the water next to the boat. Their heads bobbed above the silvery surface.

"Who comes to see us in this Genie-made boat?" they

sang in unison, their voices sounding like stringed instruments being played underwater. *"Answer quick, while you are still afloat!"*

"We've come for the sapphire," Jasmine told them. She guessed these singing fish must be the guardians of the second piece of the shattered gem. "We've found the first shard and it brought us here." She held up the sack, which let out a puff of air.

"Aha! You say you seek the shard?" sang the fish, a coy lilt in their voices. *"But against those who ask, we are on our guard."* The fish circled the boat and continued to sing. *"Three riddles we'll give. Three times you may guess. Wrong answers could doom you. But right ones pass the test."*

Jasmine nodded. "We're ready."

The fish separated to encircle the skiff. As they sang their riddles, calling out each verse, it seemed as if the words were floating up toward Jasmine and her friends from every direction:

"A grain of sand inside my mouth.
It scratches and itches. It won't come out!
It irritates. It aggravates.
Yet in the end . . . beauty it creates!"

"That doesn't make sense," said Layli.

"That's what riddles are," explained Aladdin.

Jasmine thought a moment. She liked riddles. She liked how they were puzzles with words—but she enjoyed them more when they were just for fun. Now that there was so much at stake, it was hard to concentrate.

"You start with 'sand,'" said Aladdin, continuing his explanation to Layli. "And then you go to the end: 'beauty.' Since glass can be beautiful and it's made from sand, the answer's obviously glass!" He smiled triumphantly.

"Noooo!" cooed the fish. A thunderous wave threw the boat into the air. It crashed back down onto the surface and rocked violently. Abu groaned and curled up into a ball, and even

Genie's blue skin took on a tinge of green.

Aladdin, Jasmine, and Layli held fast to the sides of the boat. A flash of panic fired through Jasmine, igniting her brain. She remembered learning that when a piece of sand lodged inside an oyster, the oyster secreted a mineral substance that surrounded it, eventually forming . . .

"A pearl!" shouted Jasmine.

"*Yeeeesssss!*" trilled the fish before launching into the next riddle:

"They can be small and narrow or big and wide.
Sometimes they live side by side.
The more of it there is, the less of it inside.
For some it is a place to live,
For others, a place to hide."

"Could be a lamp," whispered Genie.

Aladdin was skeptical. "A 'big and wide' lamp?"

Genie shrugged. "It's all relative."

"That seems too general," said Jasmine. "If

it's just a container of some kind, it could be anything—which means we could easily guess wrong. The part to think about is 'side by side.'"

Bedair flashed from inside the ring.

"Of course!" cried Genie.

"What? What did he say?" demanded Aladdin.

Jasmine glanced at Layli, who hesitated. She didn't want to guess wrong—although she believed Bedair was right. "Go on," Jasmine urged her.

Layli leaned over the side of the boat toward the fish. "Tunnels?" she said.

"Yeeeesssss!" sang the fish. *"One riddle left—win or lose! Hard or easy—we will choose!"* The fish gathered into a huddle and exchanged burbly whispers. After a moment, they separated and swam a few feet away from the boat. They rose onto their tails and crooned the final riddle:

> *"Who is he who makes the rules?*
> *Who tamed wind and rain, warm and cool?*
> *Four parts, yes, you must retrieve.*

But without his help you cannot weave.
Only he who made it first,
Can repair what's broken and break the curse."

Aladdin frowned. "This is a tricky one. Four parts of what? We need to make a list of everything that has four parts. And anything that can be woven. And then it's got to be related to wind and rain...."

Layli and Genie listened as Aladdin continued to analyze the riddle, while Jasmine smiled to herself. It was obvious to her—but could it be that easy? She glanced down at the sack with the sapphire shard, which had once again grown docile. *Yes,* she thought, *it would be that easy—for anyone who knows the legend and is here for the right reasons.*

"The Sand God!" she called out. The fish were silent. Instead of answering, they sank beneath the water: *plip-plip-plip.*

Jasmine glanced worriedly at the others. Had

she guessed wrong? Was that part of the legend made up? She'd never seen a Sand God, after all. She clutched the sack tensely, fearful that at any moment another wave would burst up and sweep the boat out to sea.

But instead, what burst from the water was a silvery geyser, on top of which perched a glistening box made of oyster shells. The geyser curved and the box slid off, landing in the bottom of the boat.

The emerald ring flashed, and Layli joined Jasmine. Together, they lifted the silver latches on the box. Jasmine handed Aladdin the sack and then carefully raised the lid, ready to catch the second shard.

It was too quick for her, however, and it leapt out of her grasp. The piece was identical to the first in size and in its elegant diamond shape. It flopped around in the bottom of the boat, much like Layli had in her carp form. Everyone dived for the piece.

Abu, who had perked up, caught it for a moment, but it quickly slipped from his hands.

"Don't let it fall in the water!" cried Jasmine as the shard bounced dangerously close to the edge of the boat. Genie flung himself at the piece, trapping it with his body. Sparks of blue light flashed beneath him and sizzled through his limbs. "*Ooh,* that tickles!" he giggled. His ponytail lit up, and his gold earring let out an energized *Ting!* before the sparks faded away.

Genie sat up, the piece now motionless in his hands. Aladdin opened the sack and Genie dropped the piece in, where it clanked against the first. The sack swung a moment, then calmed.

Jasmine noticed Genie roll his shoulders several times and tap his head. "Do you feel all right?" she asked him worriedly.

"A little *zzzz!*" replied Genie. "A bit *whoooo!* and *wowee—whoa!*" He let out a nervous huff of breath. "A big gulp of prune juice will get me right."

He snapped his fingers and held out his hand. Nothing happened. "Huh. That little dance with the sapphire must've mojoed my mojo. Let's try that again: prune juice!" Genie's palm remained empty. "One prune? . . . A raisin?" He snapped his fingers several times, but it had no effect.

Jasmine glanced at Aladdin, and he nodded sadly. It had happened again, just as it had with Carpet: Genie's magic was gone.

CHAPTER 12

"Home, sweet home!" said Genie as he led Jasmine and the others into a quaint cottage at the edge of the village, with a view of the roiling sea. "Or should I say 'Home, sweet temporary rental'? Even if I only set these two big blue feet down someplace for a week, I like my tootsies to be comfy."

"It's lovely, Genie," said Jasmine, smiling at the cozy space. Layli, who had returned to her gulin form, floated around the cottage, admiring the jewelry, flasks, and dozens of other shiny items that filled the shelves and crowded the tables.

Genie gestured to a colorful collection of satin-covered pillows scattered around the living room. "Take a seat anywhere and I'll get us warmed up in half a jiff." He crossed to the fireplace and clapped at the logs—then frowned when no spark ignited.

"I can do it," said Aladdin. He propped Magic Carpet against a wall and knelt to start the fire. Abu, eager to dry his soggy fur, hurried over to join him.

The second sapphire piece had shielded the group from the rain on their way to pick up Carpet and then to Genie's, but they had gotten so soaked in the boat that the shard's protection didn't make much difference.

Genie plopped onto a cushion to watch Aladdin stoke the glowing logs, which sent up pretty orange and yellow flames. "This 'no more magic' thing is going to take some getting used to," he said with a sigh.

Jasmine sat down next to him, setting the sack

with the shards at her feet. "I'm so sorry," she told Genie.

Genie waved the apology away as Aladdin carried Magic Carpet over to the hearth and unrolled the tapestry in front of the warm blaze. "It's not your fault," Genie told Jasmine. "There was nothing you could do."

Jasmine wasn't sure this was true. If only she'd been more alert when the piece jumped out of the box. If only she'd caught it. . . .

"You told me yourself—it was the only way to tame that crazy bouncing gem," continued Genie. "Carpet and I, we understand the importance of the hero's sacrifice, don't we?" Carpet raised a damp tassel and slapped Genie's open palm in agreement.

Jasmine studied her two magic-deprived friends nobly accepting their fate, and this made her feel even worse. She didn't want to be the kind of leader for whom others sacrificed while she sacrificed nothing. She had taken risks on this journey, but so far she had survived all of them without being required to give up anything in return.

"You're leaking again," said Layli, interrupting Jasmine's thoughts. Layli nodded to the sack at Jasmine's feet, under which a small pool of water had formed.

After they had arrived onshore and gifted the skiff to a grateful fisherman, they had noticed that the new shard occasionally let loose a spritz of water, like a miniature cloudburst. The first piece had continued to give off a puff of air now and then as well. This confirmed Ramlah's assertion that each piece of the sapphire held an atmospheric energy related to the volatile weather in the area where it had been found.

"We need to put the sack someplace where it won't get anything wet," said Jasmine.

Genie handed Aladdin some rags to mop up the puddle and then grabbed a ceramic basin from a top shelf and set it on the floor near the window. "We can hang the sack above this to catch the water," said Genie.

While Genie and Jasmine tied the sack to a hook above the basin, Layli continued inspecting Genie's collections of knickknacks. The emerald in her ring flashed. "I agree," said Layli.

The cottage reminded the siblings of their cavern in the tunnel, with its decor of shiny antiques. Genie had said he and the gulin were cousins, but it wasn't until now that Layli believed it. She picked up a copper tray engraved with a butterfly design that looked a lot like a smaller version Bedair had once brought home for her. She smiled. They were *definitely* family.

"Did you wish for all these?" Layli asked Genie.

Genie shook his head. "Bought, bartered, found by the side of the road. Wishing gets boring after a while. Of course, it was nice to have it in a pinch." He indicated some baskets in the kitchen area, filled with produce. "For instance, normally I could whip you up a feast in seconds.

But I've never actually *cooked* anything."

"Luckily, some of us have spent most of our lives making feasts of whatever we could steal— I mean *find*," said Aladdin. He summoned Abu, whose fur had dried, and the two took charge of making dinner.

While Aladdin and Abu cooked, Jasmine opened a map she had brought with her on the journey. The sack with the shards tilted on its hook, pulling gently in a direction Jasmine determined was northwest. She examined the map, which showed a wide mountain range northwest of the Gulf. However, there was no way to know if the next piece was before the mountains or after them. It could even be somewhere *in* them.

Jasmine's studying was interrupted by Aladdin's announcement that dinner was ready. The group gathered around Magic Carpet near the fire, and Aladdin and Abu handed them each a steaming bowl of hearty eggplant and lentil stew.

Layli shape-shifted into her human form to

receive her bowl. Now that she knew the joys of eating, she had no intention of skipping any opportunity to experience new tastes. She slurped up a spoonful. *"Mmm,"* she said, warmed by both the soup's heat and its spices.

Jasmine ate absentmindedly, her thoughts focused on what lay ahead. Outside the cottage window, it had gotten dark, and although the clouds covered the sky, behind them hung a nearly full moon. They had only two days left to retrieve the rest of the sapphire and return the pieces to the Sand God. She needed to know *exactly* where the next shard was so she could determine the fastest route to get there.

But how? But how? The words repeated in Jasmine's head over and over. "Oh, I don't know," she sighed to herself.

"Fresh tarragon!" said Aladdin breaking into Jasmine's thoughts. *"That's* the secret ingredient you're trying to figure out." Aladdin knew Jasmine wasn't actually talking about the stew. But he hoped teasing a smile or laugh out of her would lessen her worry, at least for a moment.

Jasmine did smile, a small pensive smile. "I'm sorry," she said. "It's delicious, Aladdin. I just wish I knew for sure what our next step should be."

The sack near the window let loose another tiny cloudburst over the basin, but that wasn't much of an answer.

"Well, as they say here: 'Only Qamar can see the future,'" said Genie.

"Qamar?" asked Jasmine. "Who's that?"

"Some recluse who lives in the woods outside the village," replied Genie.

"He's psychic?" asked Aladdin.

"*She*," corrected Genie. "I don't know exactly how she works. No one's ever actually seen her."

"Then how do you know she even exists?" asked Jasmine.

Genie shrugged. "Good point."

"None of you thought that gulin existed," Layli

pointed out. Her ring flashed in agreement.

Jasmine glanced over at Aladdin. This was true. "It's worth a try," she said. She stood and quickly carried her empty bowl to the washbasin.

"We can't go now," said Aladdin. "It's late. Some of us need a rest." He nodded toward Abu, who had snuggled himself under a corner of Carpet and was snoring softly.

"We don't have time to sleep!" protested Jasmine.

"We'll never find Qamar's place in the dark," said Genie. "And the rain's not exactly a plus."

Jasmine sighed. She didn't feel tired, but it made sense to wait. "I'm waking everyone up at dawn," she said firmly.

"Dawn it is!" said Genie, having already assembled several cushions into a bed.

"Gulin don't need sleep," said Layli. "We just sort of laze around." She glanced at Abu. "But it *does* look pleasant." She shape-shifted into a cat and curled up next to Abu on the carpet.

Aladdin gathered some cushions for Jasmine. "Here. You can have the place closest to the fire," he said.

Jasmine nodded her thanks and lay down, but her eyes remained open long after the others' had closed. *Please let this Qamar have the answer,* she silently begged as she stared out the window, willing dawn to come as quickly as possible. The *plip-plops* of the drops from the sack hitting the basin blended with the patter of the rain on the roof. The sound was soothing, but Jasmine knew she'd be awake all night.

Jasmine felt a soft tickle against her ear. It crept from her cheek to her nose. She opened her eyes—to see a spider making its way across her face.

"*Aaah!*" Jasmine burst up from the cushions, flinging away the spider, which swung across the room on a green silky thread—and shape-shifted into a giggling gulin.

"It isn't funny!" protested Jasmine. She noticed the fire was now only embers and the cloudy sky outside had lightened. Somewhere behind those clouds was the sun—she had fallen asleep! It was still raining a steady straight curtain of liquid silver.

"It is *so* funny," insisted Layli, still giggling. She wasn't alone in this opinion. Aladdin, Genie, Abu, and even Carpet were all laughing.

It was funny, thought Layli. And it felt fun. *Fun!* This is what Bedair had been telling her about, reminding her of what it had been like when gulin mixed with humans. How had the gulin thought giving this up forever was a good idea? They should have fought harder to repair things with the humans. When she got back to Agrabah, she would make sure they did.

Jasmine smiled. "All right," she conceded. "I guess it was a *little* funny. But how long have you been up?" She noticed their bags were packed.

"Why didn't you wake me?"

"We thought you'd wake up when you heard us packing," said Aladdin. "But you just kept snoring away."

"I was *not* snoring." Jasmine felt her cheeks grow warm in embarrassment.

Aladdin shared a grin with Genie. "If you say so, Your Highness," said Aladdin. "Anyway, Layli finally offered to wake you up gently."

"*Very* gentle," said Jasmine, frowning at Layli.

Layli floated toward Jasmine and shape-shifted once again into a spider, dropping down toward Jasmine's shoulder.

"*Eeek! No!*" shrieked Jasmine, racing to hide behind Genie, but she too was now laughing with the others. Layli shape-shifted to her gulin form and joined in the laughter.

Jasmine was still embarrassed about oversleeping—and snoring. It didn't seem like fit behavior for the future ruler of Agrabah. Then she remembered her father once saying, "A ruler doesn't rule alone." As they shared a quick breakfast, Jasmine gazed around at her friends, old and new. They were a good team.

CHAPTER 13

Jasmine and Aladdin agreed to leave Magic Carpet in the cottage, where he'd be safe. Then the group set out to find Qamar. It was still raining as they made their way out of the village, but the shards kept them dry.

"Then I became a snake, but I had wings and these flashing golden eyes!" Layli darted around the others, recounting the wonders of sleep. "But then I was out in the Gulf swimming with those singing fish, and I swam through a tunnel, but suddenly I was in *our* tunnels under Agrabah, but I was a panther and the tunnels were somehow aboveground in the city!"

"That's called a dream," explained Jasmine with a smile.

Layli had always thought dreams were just random thoughts that went through your mind when you were bored. "But it seemed so real!"

"That's what it feels like while you're asleep," said Aladdin.

Layli shook her head, amazed. "You mean you get to travel like this every night when you sleep? And see and be and do all these impossible things?"

"Not every time," Jasmine told her. "And you don't always remember."

"I will!" declared Layli. She had already lost centuries of opportunities for adventure. She wasn't going to give up any future experiences, real *or* imagined.

The rain lessened as they got farther away from the Gulf. By the time they reached the woods, it had slowed to a soft sprinkle. They were forced to stop when they discovered that the oak trees bordering the forest were wrapped in thick vines. The vines wound around the trees' trunks and weaved between them, as if the forest had been knitted together to form an impenetrable barrier.

"That looks like something that took more than nature to create," observed Jasmine.

"You think Qamar did this?" asked Aladdin.

"You know recluses," said Genie. "They're not big on the whole 'Come on in!' thing."

Jasmine searched the vines for an opening. "We need to figure out a way through," she said.

"Aha!" said Genie. "A lever!" He reached for a rectangular piece of wood attached to one of the trees.

"Wait," said Jasmine. "It might be a—"

"*Aah!*" cried Genie as a trapdoor opened up under him. Jasmine and Aladdin quickly dived toward him and grabbed his arms, pulling him to safety.

Aladdin pointed to similar slim wooden planks attached to several of the other trees. "There's a whole *bunch* of levers," he said. "One of them has to work. Right?" Jasmine nodded. She examined them, trying to figure out the trick. "I bet it's this one!" Aladdin pointed to a lever that was tilted slightly and was worn along one side, as if it had been used often. Before Jasmine could stop Aladdin, he pulled on it.

"*Eeeeee!*" This time it was Abu who cried out, as the patch of ground under his feet sprang up like a catapult, sending him flying back the way they had come.

Layli quickly shape-shifted into a hawk and flew after Abu. She soon returned, carrying the monkey in her beak by the scruff of his neck.

"Sorry about that, friend," said Aladdin as Layli dropped Abu into his arms. "I was wrong, I guess." Abu grumbled and pouted in reply. Layli returned to gulin form and floated down next to them.

"I think a lot of people must try that lever,"

said Jasmine. "It must be why Qamar doesn't get many—or any—visitors. They give up after being flung away. Which means it's more likely that the *right* one is the one that's been used the *least*." Jasmine spotted a lever covered in vines. She yanked away the vines and grasped the lever. The others held their breaths and took a few steps back.

"Get ready to run," Aladdin warned her.

Jasmine pulled down. There was a rustling from above and then a loud *CREEEEAK* as three of the trees bent forward like a drawbridge. Jasmine smiled.

The group made their way across the length of the trees and then stepped off onto a wide leaf-covered path. Layli floated ahead, but the others had only taken a few steps on the path when Aladdin's foot became trapped by a web of vines that had emerged from beneath the leaves. "Hey!" he said. He tugged at the vines, but this caused them to wrap around his foot even more tightly.

Jasmine moved toward Aladdin to help but

discovered that her ankle had also been grabbed by the vines. Within moments, Abu and Genie were tangled in the vines as well.

"Just give 'em a good yank," instructed Genie. He heaved on one of the vines—only to throw himself off-balance and land on his face.

"Hold on," said Layli, who had escaped the vines' clutches. "I'll free you." She shape-shifted into a beaver and chewed through the vines encircling Jasmine's ankles and then moved on to Aladdin, Genie, and Abu.

Layli was forced to repeat the action with every step the others took through the forest, returning to her gulin form whenever a vine snatched her beaver legs. It was slow going, with only Abu remaining untangled, having hopped onto Aladdin's head after Layli had freed him.

"Qamar *really* likes her privacy," grumbled Aladdin as they trudged forward.

"These traps are good signs, though," said Jasmine. "It means there is definitely someone living in these woods—someone who erected all these barriers."

The vines ended when they reached a tall, thick hedge about ten feet high.

"Now what?" asked Genie. "Climb over it?" He glanced up. "I wouldn't be surprised if there were spikes up there."

Abu chittered and pointed, tugging on Aladdin's ear, as if to steer him.

"Ow! All right, all right!" Aladdin followed Abu's direction to a spot farther down the hedge. "Hey! There's an opening here!" Aladdin pointed to a break in the hedge in front of him.

The others joined Aladdin and Abu, and the group passed through the gap, but only to find another thicket wall in front of them, with an open path to each side.

"It's a maze!" said Jasmine. Mazes were one of her favorite kinds of puzzles, but she'd only done them on paper, not in real life. She glanced left and right. Each leafy passageway seemed to go on forever, with endless possibilities for openings leading to new paths. There could be dozens of false turns and dead ends in either direction. "If we guess wrong, we could be wandering in here for hours," Jasmine told the others. "And we might not be able to find our way back."

"I guess it's up to me again!" said Layli. "Just remember: one squawk for 'right,' two squawks for 'left.'" She grinned and waved her arms, shapeshifting into a crow. She rose up and then flew out over the maze.

"Pretty handy to have a gulin along," Aladdin told Jasmine.

Jasmine nodded. "The first thing we do when we get home is bring the gulin up from the tunnels and reintroduce them to the people of Agrabah."

"*Squawk!*" Layli hovered above them, and Jasmine led the group down the path to the right. With Layli guiding, they zigged and zagged their way through the maze, until they finally emerged.

They stepped into a clearing and found a

strange, crooked mansion in front of them, with a tall bronze door flanked by two giant horses carved from ebony. The sky was completely clear here and the house was bathed in sunlight. The contrast to the gloom they'd just left was startling, and Jasmine had to squint as they approached the house.

Layli flew down to the others and returned to her gulin form as the group made their way past the horses to the house. Jasmine reached up and rang the brass bell hanging beside the door. A deep *gong* sounded from somewhere inside.

"No soliciting!" an operatic voice sang out from behind the door.

"We're not soliciting!" Jasmine called back.

"No trespassing!"

"Please," said Jasmine. "We're looking for Qamar—"

"No . . . oh, *fine.*"

The door swung open, revealing an imposing turbaned woman draped in a colorful beaded shawl. "I am Qamar," said the woman. "You obviously survived my neighbor repellants, which shows tenacity, so I suppose I should let you in, although a smarter group of"—she gazed from Jasmine and Aladdin to Genie, Abu, and Layli—"*whatever* you are would have figured out I don't like visitors."

"We're very sorry to disturb you," said Jasmine. "But it's a matter of life and death." Jasmine introduced her friends as Qamar ushered them into her dimly lit front hall. "We heard you could see the future, and—"

"What? Do I *look* like a fortune-teller?" cried Qamar.

Jasmine and the others glanced from Qamar's turban to her dangling earrings and beaded shawl. She looked *exactly* like a fortune-teller.

"Well . . . ," Jasmine began.

"I *cannot* see the future." Qamar guided the group through a long hallway and into a large room filled with glass objects of all sizes: goblets, vases, bowls, and decanters. "I *can*, however, see the present."

"See the *present*?" Aladdin whispered to Jasmine. "What good is that? *We* can do that."

"Dig this hoard!" said Genie, admiring the crowded shelves. "Puts my little trinket collection to shame." Abu hopped onto Genie's shoulder to get a closer look as well.

Layli picked up a crystal saucer. "So pretty!" she exclaimed.

"No touching!" Qamar plucked the saucer from Layli's hand. "These are very fragile and *rare*." She frowned at Layli and Genie, who scooted over next to Jasmine and Aladdin. "Now, tell me what you want and be quick about it, so I can tell you I can't help you and you'll be on your way."

Jasmine explained to Qamar about their search for the sapphire pieces and filled her in on the details of their journey so far.

"Hmm. I do recall seeing those sandstorms," said Qamar.

"You *saw* them?" asked Jasmine.

"Clear out your ears, young lady! I told you: I can see the present." Qamar picked up a glass bowl and set it on a tall table in front of her. She licked a finger and ran it around the lip of the bowl, creating a sound like the ringing of a bell. "Here we go!"

Jasmine and the others leaned in as an image appeared in the bottom of the bowl: the city of Agrabah, awash in sand, its streets deserted.

"Wow! That's incredible!" said Aladdin.

Genie agreed. "Yep—*definitely* puts my collection to shame."

"Can we see inside the palace?" Jasmine asked Qamar.

"Of course!" Qamar tilted the bowl and rubbed her finger in the other direction. A new vision of the Sultan in his throne room appeared. He was speaking with the captain of the royal guard.

"I'm afraid there's been no sign of them, Your Highness," the captain told the Sultan. "The winds have erased any tracks."

"I never should have let them go!" said the Sultan. "But Jasmine would have gone anyway." He sighed. "She's always been headstrong. Reminds me of myself at that age." He shook his head with a small smile. "She should have returned by now, unless something happened to her. . . . Yet I feel in my heart she's all right. Is that crazy?" he asked the captain.

"No!" shouted Jasmine to the bowl. "It's not crazy! I'm all right!"

"He can't hear you," said Qamar with a dismissive snort. "It's not that kind of glass."

Layli's ring flashed. "Show us the tunnels under Agrabah!" she pleaded. Qamar gave her a stern look. "Please," Layli added more softly.

Qamar tilted the bowl again and rubbed one side of the rim. The image blurred, then grew dark. It looked as if bits of dirt were falling across the view.

"What's wrong?" asked Layli. "Why can't we see it?"

The answer came from the bowl. "It's getting worse," said a voice. A hazy green shape appeared behind the falling dirt.

"That's Umab!" cried Layli.

"The sandstorms must be causing instability below, too," said Jasmine.

"Everyone is to go into the assembly cavern," continued Umab, speaking to someone they couldn't see. "It's the deepest area and the most secure. Send word to all the gulin—quickly!"

"*Hmm*," observed Qamar, setting the bowl flat and causing the image to vanish. "Seems pretty bad there."

"That's why we're here," said Jasmine, her voice taking on an urgent tone. "We need to find the rest of the sapphire. The next piece is northwest of here. If you can locate the beacon in your glass, we'll know where to go."

"Northwest? That's not very specific, is it?" said Qamar. "But I suppose that's why you felt the need to interrupt my solitude. Fine. Let's see what we can do." Qamar brought down several goblets of different sizes from the shelves and set them in a circle on the table. She ran a wet finger around each of their rims, creating a beautiful glass symphony. As she did, images appeared within each glass. Qamar gestured from the smallest glass to the largest. "These are all northwest of here. From closest to farthest away."

Jasmine and her friends studied the images. There were mountains and deserts, lakes and rivers.

Layli knew she was supposed to be searching for the star beacon, but it was difficult not to be mesmerized by the many types of landscapes, most of which she had never seen or even imagined. "What's that?" she asked, pointing to a medium-sized goblet from which tiny zigzags of light periodically blinked.

Aladdin peered down at the glass. "That's lightning," he said. "It happens sometimes, with some rainstorms." As the lightning continued, it lit up the mountaintop where the storm was raging.

"The Jahriz Mountains," said Qamar. She circled her finger around the goblet more forcefully, and the sounds of the storm emerged, including a booming *CRACK*. Layli flinched.

"That's thunder," explained Aladdin. "It's the sound the lightning makes."

Jasmine squinted more closely at the image. The sack in Jasmine's hands swung toward the glass. Was she imagining it, or ... There was another burst of lightning and, *yes,* there it was. "Look!" She pointed to a small but distinct blue shape in the sky.

"That's your beacon then, is it?" asked Qamar. "Well, good. You can be on your way. And good news! Those mountains are only about six or seven days by foot."

"Seven days?" said Jasmine, horrified. "That's too long."

"Get yourself a couple of camels and you could cut that in half," said Qamar.

Jasmine looked at Aladdin. It was still too far. "Even if both pieces are there, it'll already be too late by the time we arrive," she said. She blinked back frustrated tears. "It's hopeless."

CHAPTER 14

"So what do we do?" asked Layli.

Jasmine hesitated. She had no answer. She wondered what her father would do. She was certain he wouldn't just give up. If only they had Magic Carpet. But if Genie's magic hadn't returned, Jasmine doubted Carpet's had.

"Is there no faster way?" Jasmine asked Qamar. Jasmine assumed the answer was no, but she believed it did no harm to ask.

"I *suppose* you could borrow my horses," said

Qamar. "They could get you there by noon."

Jasmine's eyes went wide in surprise. Noon? How was that possible?

Qamar led the group back outside and gestured to the two ebony horses flanking the door.

"But . . . they're made of wood," said Aladdin.

"Wood is very sturdy material," replied Qamar. "Especially ebony. It can withstand all sorts of weather." She patted the nose of one of the horses, who instantly came to life. "This is Nabil," she said. She patted the other. "And this is Rula." The two horses snorted in greeting. "Tell them where you want to go and they'll take you there in the blink of an eye." Qamar smiled at the horses fondly. "It's been some years since they've flown. They'll probably enjoy the exercise. In my younger days, I traveled extensively, but eventually I saw quite enough of the world."

"I can't imagine *ever* seeing enough," said Layli.

Qamar smiled at Layli. "I hope you always feel that way."

Jasmine was thrilled. It had been worth asking, after all. "Since we have two horses, Genie can use one to take Carpet back to Agrabah," she told the others. "He can let Father know where we are, and that we've gotten the first two pieces of the sapphire—and will soon have the third."

Layli's ring flashed. Genie nodded. "Good idea," he told the ring.

"Bedair, are you sure?" asked Layli. The emerald glowed forcefully.

"Your brother can tell Umab everything that's happened as well," said Genie. "And check to see if the other gulin are safe."

Layli reluctantly removed the ring and handed it to Genie. It felt strange not to be wearing it—and to be separated from her brother. She rubbed her bare finger nervously.

"I'll take good care of him," Genie assured Layli.

"You should go with Genie," Aladdin told Abu. Abu chittered in protest. "You'll be safer," insisted Aladdin. "You know lightning always aims for monkeys. It's a scientific fact."

Abu narrowed his eyes suspiciously and glanced at Jasmine. She repressed a smile at Aladdin's clever lie and nodded in agreement. "It's in all the books," she said.

"And someone's got to help me keep hold of Carpet so he doesn't fall off the horse," added Genie. "Unless you think you're not up to it."

Abu glared at Genie, offended. He bent his arms, showing off his tiny biceps, and then leapt onto Nabil. Aladdin gave Genie a grateful smile.

Qamar gazed around at the group thoughtfully. "Wait here," she said. "I have a gift for you." Qamar disappeared inside and returned a few minutes later, carrying two rectangles of glass, set in wooden frames decorated with tiny black opals. She handed one to Jasmine and one to Genie. "You can communicate with each other with these—but only once each way." She indicated the single red opal on the corner of each frame. "Tap this and you will be able to see each other in the glass and speak to each other. But the image only lasts a minute, so wait until you need it. *You* will be able to initiate it once," she said to Jasmine. "And *you* once," she told Genie. "After that, they have no more magic. But they look quite nice on a shelf or table."

Qamar then handed Jasmine a straw box. "Wrapped inside here is one of my goblets. Rub the rim and the glass will show you any area within a fifty-mile radius. Once you find your next sapphire shard and know the direction of the final one, you can tilt the glass in that direction and look for your beacon. If nothing appears, use Rula to deliver you a few miles in the right direction and try again until you find it." Jasmine gave the box to Aladdin to pack. "Be careful with it," warned Qamar. "It's very fragile."

Jasmine thanked Qamar for her help and for the gifts. Despite the recluse's insistence that she did not like people, Qamar clearly had a generous heart. "We'll return the horses as soon as we can," Jasmine told her.

"No need," replied Qamar. "They'll find their way."

Genie climbed onto Nabil behind Abu and glanced down at Jasmine. "I'll check in with you as soon as we get to Agrabah—" Before he could finish, he, Abu, and Nabil became a black blur and then vanished.

Qamar shrugged. "They're very obedient."

Jasmine climbed onto Rula, the sack held tightly in her hands. Aladdin loaded up the bags. "It's going to feel strange not having a monkey sitting on my shoulder," he said.

Layli grinned and shape-shifted into a tiny green-furred capuchin. She leapt onto Aladdin's head, and he and Jasmine laughed.

Aladdin climbed onto Rula behind Jasmine. "Hold on tight!" he called out. Layli wrapped her arms around Aladdin's head. "Hey! I can't see!" he protested.

Jasmine smiled. "I guess I'll have to let you know when we get to the Jahriz Mountains."

She had barely uttered the words when Rula took off. Qamar could be heard faintly behind them, calling, "Goodbye!" as the horse soared away, flying over the forest and beyond.

Rula's legs churned but never touched the ground. The colors and hues of the world below sped past as the landscape changed from green to brown and gray to blue. Jasmine scarcely had time to catch her breath when everything stopped. They had landed, at the foot of a giant mountain covered in dark clouds.

"How do we get up there?" said Aladdin.

"Take us to the spot below the beacon," Jasmine told Rula. The horse whinnied and shook her head. Jasmine frowned. "We must need to know the exact spot." She climbed down. "We'll have to walk."

Aladdin jumped down after her. Layli leapt off his shoulder, shape-shifting to her gulin form. Aladdin had just reached for the bags when there was a deafening *CRACK!* Rula, spooked, rose onto

her hind legs, sending the bags tumbling onto the rocky ground. The ebony horse whinnied and kicked as thunder echoed around them.

"*Shhh, shhh.*" Jasmine circled Rula, stroking the horse's neck and side to calm her down.

"*. . . That's how we got here so fast. . . .*"

Jasmine glanced at Aladdin, who was as surprised as she was. It was Genie's voice they were hearing, and it was coming from inside one of the bags. Aladdin hurriedly dug through them and pulled out the frame Qamar had given them. The glass was no longer transparent. Instead, there was a blurry image of a blue-skinned arm.

"But how do you know Jasmine's all right?" asked someone Jasmine couldn't see but whose voice she knew.

She grabbed the frame from Aladdin. "Father!" she called out. "Genie!"

The blue figure turned and Genie's face filled the frame. "Hey! It works!" he said. His face backed away as he held the frame at arm's length to show the Sultan, whose worried expression transformed to wonder.

"Jasmine? Is that really you?"

"It *is*, Father, and we—"

"Did you find it already?" asked Genie, his head tilting in front of the Sultan's.

"No," replied Jasmine. "We only arrived at the mountains a second ago. Why did you contact us? Is everything all right?"

"I didn't contact you. I didn't touch the opal—genie's honor." He held up a blue palm. "You just all of a sudden appeared in the frame."

Jasmine groaned, realizing what had happened. "The bag with the frame inside it fell," she told Genie. "It must have triggered the red opal on our frame." There was nothing she could do about it now. The best thing was to use the time wisely. "Have you told Father about the gulin and the tunnels?" she asked Genie.

"He knows the whole story, and Bedair and I

are on our way there next," replied Genie. A tiny head popped into view from below—Abu. "Along with our monkey ambassador," he added. "Bedair says hello, by the way." Genie held up the ring and the emerald flashed several times.

"Yes! Yes! I'm all right!" said Layli, leaning in.

"Nabil and Carpet are both being given the royal treatment," continued Genie. "Carpet's with the royal seamstresses, who are busy rethreading all that came unraveled, and Nabil's down at the stables being fed and groomed."

The Sultan took the frame from Genie. "I want you to know how proud I am of you, Jasmine," he said. "Even though I'm worried, I know—" The image went dark.

"That's it, I guess," said Aladdin. "The minute's up."

The Sultan's words had filled Jasmine with emotion, and she found it difficult to speak. It meant so much to her to hear her father say he was proud of her, but with the happiness came fear and worry. Would he still feel the same if she failed?

But she would *not* fail. She *had* to succeed. It was as simple as that. The worry and fear would no doubt come along, but they had become familiar companions on this journey, and they had not stopped her . . . so far.

"We still have one more communication left. We'll take the frame with us and—" Jasmine was interrupted by another crack of lightning, this one louder and brighter as it lit the sky all around them.

Rula let loose a terrified *Neigh!* and vanished in a blur—just as the clouds above opened and sent down a pounding rain that blended with the thunder. The three remained dry, however, thanks to the protective energy provided by the shards.

"Rula's gone!" shouted Layli, struggling to be heard over the rain. "How will we get back to Agrabah? How will we get *anywhere?*"

"I'm sure Genie will contact us in the glass if we're not back by nightfall," yelled Jasmine. "We'll ask him to send Nabil. And we still have the goblet."

Jasmine then noticed Aladdin holding the straw box. He lifted the lid. Inside, bits of broken glass shimmered as the box filled with rain.

"What do we do now?" moaned Layli.

Jasmine took in a deep breath, determined to find the confidence she'd had only moments earlier. "We do what comes next," she said. "We climb."

CHAPTER 15

They decided to leave their bags at the base of the mountain. Layli shape-shifted into a bear and followed Jasmine and Aladdin as they began their climb up the steep, rocky slope. Jasmine carried the magic frame, wrapped inside a scarf, in a satchel around her waist. They'd agreed the frame would be safest with whoever held the shards. As before, the pieces' special atmospheric magic kept the three dry and safe from any winds.

Lightning cracked, setting fires where it

touched down, but the small spurts of rain from the sack put out any blazes nearby. Jasmine had to shield her eyes from the blinding flashes, making it impossible to search for the beacon. She had to trust the sapphire shards would lead her to it as the sack tugged her forward.

A rock dug into Layli's paw. She yanked it up and licked it, her moan muffled by the storm. She wasn't used to pain. She hadn't forgotten that gulin were vulnerable in their shape-shifted forms, but in the two days since she'd left the tunnels, she had been able to handle it.

Layli felt the rain pelt her fur and discovered she'd fallen behind Jasmine and Aladdin, out of the shards' protective shell. She hurried to catch up. As she did, a bolt of lightning hit a nearby tree, slicing it in half. The severed trunk toppled, its bark sizzling as the rain hit the charred wood.

"Look out!" shouted Jasmine as she darted out of the way. Aladdin, startled, stumbled on a rock. Jasmine reached for him, but the sack pulled against her. Aladdin tumbled into Layli and the two slid backward, somersaulting down the path. Jasmine tried to go after them, but the power of the shards was too great.

"Jasmine! Look up!" called Aladdin from somewhere below. Jasmine glanced above her and caught a glimpse of the star through the trees. It cast a blue light toward the ground ahead. "Go!" Aladdin shouted.

Jasmine yelled down to him, "Are you hurt?"

"I'm all right!" he insisted. "Go get the piece!"

"Go!" echoed Layli's voice from somewhere closer to Jasmine, yet still out of sight. "I'll find Aladdin, and we'll catch up!"

Jasmine hesitated. Should she go back or continue on? Why did it seem as if every decision was more difficult than the last? Why was it that every time she felt sure, something would happen to flood her with new doubts? Would it be like this when she ruled Agrabah? Would everything become harder rather than easier as time went on?

Even as Jasmine's mind wavered, her feet seemed to have made the choice. Step by step, she was moving forward, upward, toward the beacon.

Jasmine arrived at a giant boulder. The beacon beamed straight down onto it, shrouding it in a blue glow. The sky, as in the Gulf, was clear around the beacon, and below was an area free of rain.

A tall, willowy woman emerged from behind the boulder. She wore a gown woven of black and brown threads, and silver needle-shaped earrings hung from her ears. Her long black hair was held back by a shimmery forest-green scarf. "I am Kinza!" she shouted after a new round of thunder. "And you must be Princess Jasmine!"

"How did you—"

"Wait a moment!" Kinza waved her arms. The boulder dissolved into a mist of gray specks, which flew up and then rained down, creating a transparent protective shell. Jasmine reached out and touched the clear wall. It was smooth like glass but had a soft, watery feel, like velvet.

The sphere blocked out all sound from the storm. "There," said Kinza. "That's better. Now we can converse in a civilized tone." She stared down at Jasmine coolly. "I know who you are because Ramlah and I keep in touch." She tapped her temple. "She told me of the visit you had with her—and I see you've acquired another piece of the sapphire as well." Kinza nodded to the sack in Jasmine's hand. "Soon, perhaps, you'll have your third—once you pass the test."

Kinza waved her arms again and seven paintings appeared on the invisible wall surrounding them, as if suspended in midair, creating a circular art gallery. "Each painting has a name," said Kinza. She circled the space, her gown trailing elegantly behind her. "Answer correctly and the picture will come alive and produce a clue to the title of the next painting. Answer incorrectly and another, more complicated image will appear in its place."

Jasmine sighed, weary at the thought of having to solve another puzzle. She was hungry and tired, and overwhelmed with worry about Aladdin and Layli. She struggled to shake off her exhaustion as Kinza continued. "Once you have correctly guessed all the paintings' titles, the first letter of each answer will provide a *final* puzzle," said Kinza. "Solve that and the sapphire shard will emerge." Kinza glanced around as if searching for something outside the clear dome. "You will need your gulin companion, too."

"She's on her way," said Jasmine, hoping this was true.

"Hmm. Well, you only need her to free the piece, not to solve the puzzle," conceded Kinza. "Since I have no intention of standing around and waiting, you might as well begin." She gestured to the first painting.

Jasmine nodded. She had no choice but to do her best—and to try to block out her concern about Layli and Aladdin.

◆◆◆◆

Aladdin leaned against the base of a tree and massaged his ankle. He'd tried to stand, but it was too painful. He heard a growl and glanced up in fright—but then noticed the green tint to the fur of the bear lumbering toward him. "What are you doing down here?" he asked Layli. "You need to get back to Jasmine. She can't retrieve the piece without you."

Layli shape-shifted back to her gulin form. "I know where she is. I saw the guardian. I'll go as soon as we find you better shelter."

"I can't walk." Aladdin nodded to his ankle. "I think I broke it."

Layli spotted several felled trees that had collapsed against each other a few feet behind Aladdin. "I'll help you," she said, shape-shifting into a human. Aladdin put an arm over her shoulder and she guided him up to a standing position, and then helped him limp down to the makeshift tent.

Once Aladdin had settled in safely under the

trees, he gestured to Layli to go. "I'll be fine," he said.

"We'll be back soon," promised Layli, and then she transformed into a lynx. Her muscular feline body allowed her to dash quickly up the muddy, rocky path. Again, as when she had left the tunnels and later flown above the Gulf, her gulin sensibility connected with the magic in the air, which grew stronger the closer she got to the beacon.

CHAPTER
16

While Layli was helping Aladdin, Jasmine was studying the first painting. It depicted a landscape—a jagged mountain range. It wasn't the Jahriz Mountains. Its snowy peaks were a different shape than those she had seen in Qamar's glass. But if not here, where? Was she expected to know every mountain range in the world? Should she guess and risk making the puzzle more difficult? Her weariness and frustration made it hard to focus. "I don't know!" she said. "The Ahmar

Mountains, the Sumuun Mountains, the—"

"That's enough," Kinza said abruptly, waving her hand toward the painting. "You're wrong about the range. It's somewhere in India, I believe. But 'Mountains' is the answer."

The painting came to life, just as the guardian had said it would if Jasmine guessed correctly. The image tilted and then moved, as if it were the point of view of a bird in flight. It soared downward, revealing a ribbon of blue flowing water at the base of the mountain. The painting vanished and Jasmine's eyes were drawn to the frame next to it, inside of which was a painting of another ribbon of blue, this one dominating the image.

The title of the first painting had been easier to guess than Jasmine had expected. Would they all be so simple? "River?" she asked tentatively.

"Don't be so half-hearted about it," said Kinza with a disapproving frown. "It shows a lack of self-assurance. Right or wrong, it's better to be bold than meek. But to answer your question . . . *look*."

Kinza pointed to the painting, which had, like the first, come alive. "You are correct. 'River' is the title." Inside the frame, the view followed the river out to the sea. This painting, too, vanished and Jasmine moved to the next, which was an endless expanse of watery blue. "Ocean," said Jasmine.

Kinza nodded, and Jasmine was able to guess the next two titles within seconds: "Hills. . . . Animals," she said, growing more assured with each one.

She reached the second to last painting to find not a single image but several tiny oval portraits arranged in a spiral within the frame. Each oval showed a miniature view of the previous paintings. Jasmine was thrown for a moment, but then she noticed there were no cities or buildings in any of the images. Everything was part of . . .

"Nature," said Jasmine.

"Very good," said Kinza. "I'm quite impressed. One more."

The tiny paintings spun within their frame,

then floated out from it, blending together and landing inside the final frame to become a single wide view of a gorgeous vista.

This painting was alive from the start, and Jasmine watched as its sun rose and fell, faster and faster. Green leaves turned to yellow, then red, then brown, finally falling, revealing bare branches. Snow appeared on mountaintops, lakes froze and then melted, and greens again dotted the hills and trees.

"Seasons!" declared Jasmine. The painting instantly went dark.

"I'm afraid not," said Kinza, shaking her head. "Boldly said, though. Try again."

A new image appeared: a single rock on a sandy shore. Night and day blinked on and off against its gray surface. Water washed up past the rock and then receded, over and over. What could it mean?

Jasmine closed her eyes and took a breath, something she often did when she had reached a particularly difficult question in her lessons at the palace. She remembered what Kinza had said about the first letter of each answer creating a final puzzle. Jasmine pictured the letters she had so far: M-R-O-H-A-N. . . . Then she rearranged them in her mind. R-A-M-H-O-N . . . H-A-R—

Jasmine opened her eyes. She knew the final word, and she needed a Y to spell it. The rock in the painting fell into darkness again as another night passed, and more sand eroded away.

"Years," said Jasmine.

Kinza smiled approvingly and waved her arms one last time. The images from all the paintings reappeared and wove together, creating a giant mural that spanned the inside of the dome. Jasmine looked at it—it was the earth, all lands blending together. A vision of the world in . . .

"Harmony," said Jasmine.

"'Harmony' indeed," said Kinza. "That's what we are all here for, is it not? To restore harmony to the kingdom?" She tapped a foot on the ground and a box rose up, carved from beechwood, with two tarnished copper clasps. "However, I'm afraid we now have to wait until— Ah! There she is!"

Jasmine followed Kinza's gaze to see a green-furred lynx tapping a paw against the outside of the dome. Kinza clapped her hands and the dome vanished, allowing Layli to enter, shape-shifting into her human form as she did.

"My work here is completed," Kinza told Jasmine and Layli. "It is up to you two now to complete your quest. And I have a long-planned lunch date with Ramlah." A distant flash of lightning lit up the clouds as Kinza raised her arms and vanished.

Thunder rumbled above them as Jasmine met Layli's gaze. They'd both seen the danger in letting the volatile shard loose too quickly. "We need a strategy," said Jasmine. "I'll line the top of the sack against the space between the lid and the base of the box. After we unlock it, you slowly raise the lid and I'll catch the piece as it flies out."

Layli nodded. "I'm ready," she said. Jasmine

loosened the strings on the top of the sack and pressed it against the box with one hand, between the two clasps. Together, she and Layli carefully lifted the latches.

Jasmine then put both hands on the sack and stretched the opening as far across the width of the box as it would go. Layli grasped a corner of the lid and began to lift. Jasmine tensed, determined to capture the piece the moment it rose up.

Suddenly, a bright bolt of lightning struck the ground a few feet away from them. Startled, Layli lost her grip on the lid. The diamond-shaped sapphire shard burst up, escaping Jasmine's trap, and leapt away.

Layli dived after it, but it jumped free, bouncing down the mountain.

"We can't lose it!" shouted Jasmine as she joined Layli. They raced after the fleeing shard and tried not to stumble on the rocky path.

Layli knew what she had to do. Her gulin instinct took over as she shape-shifted into a bat.

The clouds had thickened, completely blocking out the sun, and the canopy of trees made it even darker. Yet Layli's nocturnal vision was crisp and clear, and she was able to see the shard as it attempted to escape. She swooped down, wings wide, and landed on top of it.

Jasmine had lost sight of Layli and the shard, but she saw sparks illuminating an area of the forest below her. She heard the pops and sizzles as she grew closer. When she arrived, she found a bat facedown on the ground, a dim blue glow emerging from underneath its body.

"Layli?" whispered Jasmine. The bat raised a wing and gestured to its stomach. Jasmine knelt, and she and the bat scooped the shard into the sack with the other two pieces.

The bat flopped onto its back and blinked its dazed eyes. Jasmine regarded her friend worriedly. "Are you all right?"

Layli flapped her wings and was able to rise.

She circled Jasmine's head a few times—but remained a bat. She could fly fine. But she could no longer shape-shift. She was trapped in her bat form, perhaps forever.

CHAPTER 17

"You won't remain a bat for long," Jasmine assured Layli, sensing Layli's thoughts as they made their way down the mountain toward Aladdin. The sack tugged Jasmine along, giving off small bursts of light, allowing her to see the path ahead. "Once we restore the sapphire—"

Lightning cracked nearby and Layli flew lower in order to stay inside the shards' protective aura. Layli realized Jasmine was trying to make her feel better. But, like Layli, Jasmine could not truly know what would happen with her magic—or if they'd even find the last sapphire piece in time.

Layli felt a pang of sadness at the thought of giving up all the wondrous possibilities that came with being a gulin—just when she'd finally discovered and embraced them. But if she had let the shard get away, those possibilities would have been lost anyway. If she had to remain a bat, she would be sure to live the most exciting, adventurous life of any bat ever.

Layli spotted Aladdin under the tented tree trunks, his face illuminated by a strange light from below. She swooped down in front of Jasmine and flapped a wing in Aladdin's direction.

Jasmine followed Layli. As they grew closer, they could hear two voices. Aladdin's and . . .

"Where is Layli?" demanded the other voice.

Bedair! Layli sailed ahead, not caring about the storm. She reached Aladdin, who was holding Qamar's magic frame in his lap.

Layli dived toward Aladdin, who cried out,

startled. "Ah! Go away!" He waved an arm at her as she swooped around him, trying to get closer. "Get out!"

"Stop!" yelled Jasmine, hurrying to catch up. "It's Layli!"

"Layli?" Bedair's voice rose from the glass. Jasmine crouched next to Aladdin, and Layli landed on her shoulder.

"Layli trapped the piece, and it absorbed her magic, like with Genie and Carpet," explained Jasmine.

"Wow. That's rough," said Genie as he appeared in the glass next to Bedair. "Sorry to hear it, Layli. At least you're in good compan—" He was interrupted by a rumble. Bits of red clay fell through the framed image.

"The earthquakes have gotten worse," said Bedair. "Falling rocks have blocked all the exits from the cavern. Even if we shape-shifted into ants, we'd never make it through. The rocks move with every quake. We'd be crushed."

"Aladdin gave me the scoop about Rula," said Genie. "But unfortunately, Nabil is still at the palace and there's no way for us to send word up there."

Before Jasmine even had a chance to react to this information, Layli let out a tiny squeak and pointed her wing at the glass. A spot in the wall behind Genie and Bedair seem to be glowing—a bright shade of blue.

"It can't be," said Jasmine. "The beacon?"

"Where? Where?" said Genie. The image shifted and a blur of browns and greens whipped through the frame as the view moved quickly past the rocks and walls and gulin, stopping finally at a familiar star-shape emerging from the clay. "Well, I'll be!" Jasmine heard Genie say as he kept the frame focused on the shape, which grew bigger as he approached it. "It was here all along!"

"Why hasn't the guardian appeared?" asked Aladdin. "You only need a gulin and a human to open the box, right? Not to take the test."

"Layli wasn't with me when Kinza appeared,"

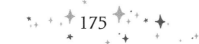

agreed Jasmine. "But she wasn't far away. There isn't a human in the tunnels, or nearby. We need to get back there."

The image in the glass shook again, this time more violently. Falling rocks filled the view. "*Ooeee!*" said Genie. "That was a big one!"

"Stay safe!" Jasmine shouted to the glass. "We're on our way—" The image vanished.

Aladdin looked up from the darkened frame. "How do we get to Agrabah without Nabil?" he asked Jasmine.

"We'll find a way." Jasmine grabbed a fallen branch and handed it to Aladdin to use as a crutch. "We retrieved the first three pieces thanks to assistance we received that we never could have predicted." She helped Aladdin to his feet and they started down the mountain, with Layli flying over-head. "More strokes of luck may lie ahead. As long as we keep moving forward."

"I guess you're right," said Aladdin. The new shard's tiny lightning bursts illuminated their path.

"It *was* lucky I fell so far down the mountain. Makes for a shorter walk."

Jasmine laughed. And it was true. They soon arrived at the tree where they had left the bags. The storm still raged above them, but their belongings were dry.

Jasmine picked up the bags and stepped out from under the tree's shade. Aladdin followed. Layli landed on Jasmine's shoulder and quickly folded her wings around her to protect her sensitive eyes from the daylight.

"We know Agrabah is to the east," said Jasmine. She gazed toward the setting sun hanging low over the horizon, and a flutter of panic rose in her chest. The full moon would rise within hours.

"Maybe we'll meet another nomad family," said Aladdin, sensing her fears.

Jasmine met his gaze with a smile. "With a very fast camel," she added.

"A magic *flying* camel!" suggested Aladdin.

Jasmine grinned. "It's possible! We didn't expect

a magical flying horse, did we?" Layli peeped from beneath her wings in agreement.

Aladdin grinned. "We sure—"

A large black object suddenly appeared in front of him: a giant ebony horse.

Aladdin let out an amazed laugh as he finished his thought: "—*didn't*."

"Rula!" cried Jasmine. "You came back!"

Rula lowered her head. Clutched in her mouth was a small pouch, which she held out to Jasmine. Jasmine took it and opened it. Inside was a tiny glass frame with a single red opal in one corner. Jasmine tapped the gem and Qamar appeared in the glass.

"Ah! There you are! Wonderful!" said Qamar. "When Rula came back, I assumed you'd completed your quest, but then I discovered the weather problems throughout the land were continuing. When Nabil did not return, I finally decided to check up on you in my bowl. I'd never tried sending one of the horses without a rider, so I didn't know if it would work, but I must admit, I'm quite glad to see—"

The frame went dark.

Aladdin shrugged. "I guess the small frames don't last as long."

Rula whinnied and lowered her forelegs to make it easier for Jasmine and Aladdin to climb on. Layli flew down to land on Rula's neck and clutched the horse's mane in her claws.

When Jasmine was certain everyone was holding on tight, she called out her request to Rula: "Take us to Agrabah!"

CHAPTER 18

The ground beneath Jasmine vanished. Soon the crimson sky blurred and then disappeared, absorbed within the dusty cloud cover of the sandstorm.

They landed outside the palace. The marketplace was eerily deserted and twisters of sand spun through the empty streets, as if taking part in a strange tornado dance. The sand steered clear of Jasmine and her friends, however, thanks to the shards. They had left only three days before, but it seemed to Jasmine as if months had passed, due to all that had happened.

The ground shook beneath them, interrupting her thoughts. A few stones from the top of the palace walls were jostled free. Rula quickly stepped out of their path. "The earthquakes," said Aladdin. They both glanced down, knowing the shaking was much worse in the tunnels below. Layli flapped a wing, worried.

"We'll be there soon," Jasmine assured her.

Aladdin stayed on Rula as Jasmine led the horse to the royal stables, with Layli flying above. After leaving Rula with Nabil, Jasmine asked one of the guards to help Aladdin to the infirmary. Then, clutching the sack of shards and carrying Layli in her other hand, Jasmine hurried inside to find her father.

In the throne room, the Sultan paced. "You're certain no one remains trapped by any fallen debris?" he asked the captain of the guard.

"Yes, Your Highness," replied the captain. "Everyone has kept watch over their neighbors since the storms began. Anyone living alone had two or three people checking on them. This was how we were able to find and rescue the few who had been trapped."

"Good, good," said the Sultan. "And is everyone in the shelters receiving adequate medical care?"

"Yes, Your—"

"Father!"

The Sultan's eyes went wide as Jasmine rushed into the room. Her father hurried toward her and the two embraced—or tried to. Jasmine still held the sack, as well as Layli, who squeaked in protest as she was crushed between father and daughter.

"I'm sorry! Are you all right?" Jasmine peered worriedly at Layli, who peeked out from under a wing and squinted at the bright light from the torches along the walls.

"This is Layli," Jasmine told her father, and then she explained how her friend had become trapped in her current form.

"I met your brother," said the Sultan, addressing the tiny bat. "Although he was . . . an emerald."

"You'll be able to meet both of them in their proper gulin form once we've restored the sapphire," said Jasmine, determined to reassure Layli whenever possible.

"You've found it, then!" The Sultan glanced at the sack, which let out a puff of air and a flash of light.

"*Almost*," said Jasmine. "There's one more piece. And it's here in the city—or rather, under it. We'll need a few of your guards and tools to dig with."

The Sultan nodded and instructed the captain of the guard to assemble a team. He then accompanied Jasmine through the halls to the infirmary.

Aladdin's ankle was now in a splint, and he had been given two proper crutches. He'd also been reunited with Abu, who had his arms wrapped tightly around Aladdin's neck.

"He missed me," Aladdin said with a grin as Jasmine and the Sultan approached. Abu shrugged and pursed his lips as if to say, *Ha! Not really.* But then the little monkey hugged Aladdin even tighter.

"*Cho . . . king . . .*," gasped Aladdin. Abu loosened his grip slightly.

Jasmine gestured to Aladdin's wrapped ankle. "You should probably stay—"

"Oh no," said Aladdin. "I'm coming along." He coughed as Abu gave him another squeeze. "*Abu . . . too . . .*"

"I'll come as well," added the Sultan.

"No, Father," insisted Jasmine. "Your place is here in the palace."

"Jasmine—"

Jasmine put a hand on her father's arm, interrupting him. "As the future ruler of Agrabah, I would like to ask your advice, Your Highness," she said. "If I were in your place in a situation such as this, would you tell me to leave my post, my responsibilities to the citizens of my city, in order to take on a task that another has proved herself capable of achieving?"

The Sultan studied Jasmine sternly for a moment, then shook his head. "When did you get so smart?" he asked.

Jasmine smiled. "It came from spending my life studying the actions of the wisest and bravest man I know."

"Wow! I'm flattered!" said Aladdin. "Although, you haven't actually known me your *whole* life."

Jasmine and the Sultan laughed. But the mood among all three of them soon grew serious again as they focused on the work that lay ahead.

Jasmine, Aladdin, Layli, and Abu met up with the team of guards at the palace gates. The windswept sky had darkened as dusk descended, warning

Jasmine that the moon would soon be rising—not that she needed reminding. The protective power of the shards expanded to shelter the guards, Jasmine, and her friends as they passed through the city to the entrance to the tunnels.

Once inside the tunnels, Layli flew up and hovered over the group, able to see clearly again now that they were in the dark. Lightning bursts from the sack lit the way for the others.

The path was initially clear and they made good time as they descended under the city, but eventually they arrived at one of the cave-ins and the digging began. Again, the shards helped, spritzing water to dampen clumps of dirt and emitting puffs of air to blow away debris. Now and then a rumble from the earthquakes below would shake the walls and ceiling of the passageway. But the rocks and dirt fell around them rather than onto them, thanks to the sapphire pieces. When they reached a fork, and the tunnel split into two or more paths, the sack guided them, pulling

Jasmine in the direction they needed to go.

Eventually Jasmine and the others could hear voices, and they dug their way into a large cavern, crowded with green-skinned gulin of all sizes. The guards gaped at the wraithlike figures, who huddled closely together, regarding the invaders warily. Among the green, one blue-skinned figure stood out.

"Genie!" cried Aladdin.

Genie had already crossed toward them. "You made it—"

A fierce rumble shook the cavern. The guards, still standing in the entrance, rushed into the room as rubble fell, closing off the passageway they had just dug through.

Jasmine noticed the room was lit by a green glow, not from the gulin, but from the tiny pool in the bottom of the grotto to her left. She peered in and saw two luminescent jellyfish in the water. "That's Misk and Luli," said Genie. "They shape-shifted so I could see inside the cavern."

"Gulin can see in the dark," explained Bedair, who had joined the group. Layli peeped and fluttered down to land on his shoulder. Seeing Bedair restored to his gulin form canceled out any regret she still felt at losing her ability to shape-shift. "And bats, too," he added. He stroked Layli's head sadly. "Layli ... I'm so sorry."

Layli squeaked and flapped her wings in protest. She peeped several times, a few long peeps interspersed with slow ones: an aural version of their code.

"Yes, we can definitely have adventures no matter what," agreed Bedair. "We can even be bats together!" Bedair shape-shifted into a bat and flapped up next to Layli. They circled around each other, squeaking and playfully slapping wings.

"Bedair!" A tall gulin floated across the cavern, the other gulin quickly clearing space for her. "This is *not* a time for fun and games!"

Bedair returned to his gulin form. "I'm sorry, Umab."

Umab turned to Jasmine. "You must be Princess Jasmine," she said as she shape-shifted into a human queen and held out her hand.

Jasmine took Umab's hand and shook it. "It's an honor to meet you."

"The honor is mine," insisted Umab. "As is the apology I must offer for my part in delaying the recovery of the sapphire for all these years." Umab gestured at a pile of rubble at the base of one wall. "This could have all been avoided. But my full apology can come later, once you've retrieved the final shard. I hope you can. I'm afraid we have not had much luck."

Jasmine was confused. Had the final guardian emerged? She glanced around the cavern, searching. Umab again gestured to the rubble and Jasmine now saw, in the dim green light, the faint blue star shape in the clay wall above the rocks: the beacon.

CHAPTER 19

Jasmine gestured to one of the guards. "Bring your shovel. We'll try digging through—"

"Pardon me?" growled a voice from inside the rubble. "Get that shovel away from me!" The guard quickly stepped back as the rubble shifted and seemed to unfold. Bits of rock dropped away, revealing a creature made of clay—a figurine come to life.

"Oh! I'm sorry!" exclaimed Jasmine. The sack tugged at Jasmine's hands and swung toward the creature, and Jasmine realized this was the last guardian.

"And get *that* away from me as well!" the clay figure snapped.

"These are the other pieces of the sapphire," explained Jasmine. "We just need the last. The one you—"

"Do you think I don't know all *that?*" the creature grumbled in his gravelly voice. "I already told your friends here. . . ." He waved toward the gulin, and bits of clay flew off his arms. "It's too late."

"Not yet," insisted Jasmine. "The moon hasn't ris—"

"Oh, moon, croon, maroon—what do I care about the moon? I, Turab, have been stuck in this wall for a thousand years while you fools wasted time."

"We're here now," said Jasmine. "We're ready to solve the puzzle."

"Ha! I never bothered with that," snorted Turab. "There's no test. I didn't want this job in the first place—but you can't say no to the Sand God!" The walls trembled as another quake hit. Dirt fell onto Turab but was absorbed into his clay body. "I was only too willing to give the piece to the first human-gulin pair who came looking," he went on, barely noticing the quake. "I thought it would take a few weeks at most, maybe a couple of months— *Ha!*"

"But if there's no test, couldn't you just—"

"No, I could not *just*," sneered Turab, mocking Jasmine. "You didn't even bother to look in your own kingdom first! When *I* had the closest piece! Last in everything, that's what I am and have always been. Forgotten and overlooked. Let your land crumble to dust—*I'll* still be here when it's all over." Turab folded his arms and they seemed to disappear into his torso. He pouted, and his lips were also absorbed by the clay.

All eyes were on Jasmine, as the gulin, humans, Genie, and Abu waited for her next move.

Jasmine was silent for a moment. Turab was

wrong when he'd said there was no test, she realized. *This* was the test: not a puzzle, but a person.

Jasmine thought about how she had persuaded Qamar to help them by appealing to the recluse's sympathy, how she had convinced her father to remain behind by being firm and committed, and how she had led the guards through the tunnels by being calm and self-assured. She had done these things instinctively, but she now saw that in each case she had acted in a way that was most effective for the personalities she was dealing with.

Turab was angry, yet under that anger was hurt, due to his belief that he had been neglected and ignored—that he had been forgotten.

That was the key. Jasmine knew what to do.

"Yes, you may still be here if the tunnels collapse, and if the storms raging across the kingdom destroy everything and everyone above," Jasmine told Turab. "But then you'll never have a chance to be a hero. You'll never go down in history as someone as famous or admired as the Sand God—because there will be no one left to record that history."

Turab shifted. His lips reappeared. "Hero?" he asked doubtfully.

"Of course!" said Jasmine. "You would be the guardian who guarded a piece of the sapphire the longest and saved the kingdom at the last possible moment."

Turab thought this over. "How do I know I can trust you?" he asked Jasmine.

"I promise you everything I'm saying is true," said Jasmine. "But you don't really need that promise, because I'm simply stating the facts—if you help."

Turab emitted a small grunt and dissolved into the wall. Jasmine felt a brief moment of uncertainty. Had she judged wrong? But then, a moment later, Turab reemerged, now holding a ceramic box with two closures made of twine.

Jasmine sighed in relief and hurried to the

box, joined by Bedair, with Layli on his shoulder. Jasmine and Bedair lifted the twine latches.

"We need to surround the box," Jasmine told Aladdin and Genie. "I don't want anyone else to have to sacrifice their magic." She gestured for Bedair to back away as Aladdin limped over, accompanied by Genie.

Jasmine nodded to Aladdin, who held the sack open as she slowly lifted the lid of the box. Genie threw his big arms wide, ready to grab the shard if necessary. The piece flew straight up—and into the sack!

The others cheered—but the sack yanked at Aladdin, and he lost his balance, tumbling backward as his crutches fell. The fourth piece of the sapphire exploded out of the sack and zipped around the cavern, bouncing off the walls and causing more debris to fall.

The guards ducked and the gulin darted out of the way as Jasmine, Genie, and Abu chased after the sapphire shard. Bedair glanced up at Layli and they exchanged a nod. Bedair shape-shifted into a bat. He flew toward the piece, but just as he was swooping down, the queenly figure of Umab came into view and she pulled the piece into a tight embrace. She clutched the shard to her stomach as sparks flickered through her body and through her green embroidered silk dress.

Jasmine stared in awe at the gulin leader's sacrifice. The piece calmed and Umab dropped it into the sack, now in Jasmine's hands. "It was only right that it be me," said Umab.

Turab scowled. "I guess *you're* the true hero now," he grumbled.

"No," replied Umab. "There are many heroes here." She smiled at Layli and Genie, and then at Jasmine and Aladdin. "Besides, being trapped as a human queen is not all that bad, I don't think." She smiled. "But if we are all to be hailed as heroes, we need to work together to finish what Princess Jasmine started."

Bedair nodded. "We need to take the pieces

to the Sand God, in the desert outside the city."
Bedair explained that he and his friend Niddal
had sought out the Sand God after they had
accidentally broken the sapphire, to find out what
could be done. It was then that the Sand God
had delayed the curse for a thousand years, to
give the gulin and humans time to retrieve the
shattered pieces.

"We'll need to dig our way out of here," said
Jasmine. Bedair pointed to another cavern
entrance that had been blocked off, which led
directly to the desert. Jasmine gestured to the
guards, who began to dig into the rubble with their
shovels. Abu and Genie quickly joined in, pick-
ing up rocks and moving them out of the way.
The shards, now reunited, spun around inside the
sack, as if trying to reform. Jasmine could hear
them clanking against each other, and she had
to use all her strength to hold onto the sack and
prevent it from pulling free of her grasp.

"If any of you is willing to help, it will speed up

the task," Jasmine told the gulin. "I know shape-shifting could make you vulnerable to the falling debris, so I understand if you say no."

Bedair instantly shape-shifted into a wolf and joined the digging as Layli flew above him, flapping her wings and urging him on.

"My gulin," said Umab to the hesitant green wraiths watching the activity from their huddled groups. "The true danger lies in a future of chaos. Not only will we lose any chance for a reunion with the human world, but our tunnels are collapsing, and even if we remain in gulin form, we may well be blown to the winds anyway, scattered in all directions." She cast her eyes around at the group, her expression both encouraging and pleading. "As a human, I will do what I can," she said. "Will you join me? Will you join our friends? Will you fight for a peaceful, joyful future?"

Jasmine was as moved by Umab's speech as the gulin were, and she watched, grateful, as one by one they shape-shifted, becoming wolves, mole rats, voles, and raccoons. They dug alongside the guards while Umab joined Abu and Genie. Working together, they soon broke through and began making their way to the desert above.

"Maybe try an animal that actually fits into a tunnel," said Aladdin to the last gulin. It was one of the jellyfish, who had left the pool and shapeshifted into an elephant, which took up half the near-empty cavern.

The gulin thought a moment and then transformed into a monkey, racing to join Abu. Aladdin smiled. He limped after the others, leaving the dark cavern, now completely empty, behind.

Jasmine walked alongside the group, organizing animals and humans into more efficient teams. The fourth sapphire piece, like the first three, emitted a protective energy, one that shielded anyone nearby from falling rocks. This was occasionally accompanied by a small cloud of dust from the final piece, but the first shard's puff of air quickly blew the dust away.

As they continued on, Jasmine held the sack high, using the shards' power to protect her army. *Her army* . . . that's what they had become as they worked together, fighting rock and weariness and time. *This* was the best use of an army, she believed: to help, not harm.

They emerged at last into the desert. The moon shone brightly, far above the horizon, but not yet directly overhead, casting a gorgeous shimmer across the sand.

The sandstorms had calmed, but it was an eerie calm, a frightening silence, as if some terrifying power was gathering its strength and would, at any moment, let loose. . . .

CHAPTER
20

Bedair led the group to the spot where he and Niddal had met the Sand God one thousand years earlier. "We're here!" he called out to the indigo sky.

"We have the sapphire pieces!" shouted Jasmine. She lifted the sack of shards, which were no longer giving any sign of the unique atmospheric energies they had emitted throughout the journey.

Jasmine and the others waited. Each minute

felt like hours. Although it remained calm where they stood, Jasmine could see signs of the sandstorms farther out in the desert, as if waiting for the right moment to return.

"Where is he?" asked Umab.

"Yo! Sandy!" shouted Genie. "Come out, come out, wherever you are!"

"It's been a thousand years," said Turab. "He may have given up. Maybe he's not even here anymore."

Jasmine shook her head, refusing to accept this. "That can't be true," she said. "Not after everything we've been through." She stared up at the moon. *Had* it all been for nothing? She had experienced so many setbacks throughout their journey, but this would truly be the worst a leader could ever face: to have done everything she could and still have failed.

No doubt in the future, she *would* fail now and then. It was inevitable. But not today. Today she had to be right. "I have an idea," she said. She carefully loosened the strings on the sack.

"What are you doing?" cried Aladdin. "They'll fly away!"

"'Since a human and a gulin were responsible for shattering the sapphire, a human and a gulin must be present to unlock each shard from its hiding place,'" said Jasmine, repeating Ramlah's words from two days before. Jasmine thought for a moment. "So . . . maybe a human and a gulin must work together to restore it. Or, better yet, *two* humans and *two* gulin."

Jasmine handed a shard each to Aladdin and Bedair, and helped Layli, who had flown down to the sand, clutch a third piece between her wings. Jasmine took the fourth shard in her own hands. It was as smooth as glass and cool to the touch.

"Let's try to put them together ourselves," Jasmine told the others. "Whatever energy propelled us from one piece to the next might help them re-form." She held out her shard. "Point one of the tips forward." The others followed

Jasmine's direction. "Now we'll place them against each other...."

Jasmine and her friends pressed the shards together, forming a four-pointed sapphire star. The pieces began to glow, as if a flame had been lit inside of them.

"*Whoa!*" said Aladdin when the light in his piece grew stronger and brighter.

"It's vibrating!" shouted Bedair.

Jasmine could feel it as well. This energy was different from any she had felt on the journey so far. It was a gentle buzz at first, but, like the glow, it increased until the piece was shaking so fiercely in her hands, it was all she could do to keep hold of it. Layli, too, clung tightly to her shard, hugging her wings around it, her small bat body shaking along with the piece.

The light from inside the shards became so bright, Jasmine and her friends had to close their eyes. Layli squeaked as the piece she held burst out of her grasp. The other pieces flew free as well, and Genie, Abu, Umab, and the other gulin gasped in horror.

"No!" cried Umab.

"Wait." Jasmine held out an arm to calm the group. "Look!" She pointed up to where the pieces were now slowly rotating around each other, sending off sparks of magical dust.

Beneath the spinning shards, a cyclone of sand rose from the desert floor and swirled into a towering form. Arms of sand emerged from the form and then a head. Two eyes, as bright as stars, blinked open.

"The Sand God," said Aladdin, his voice hushed with awe.

The buzzing Jasmine had felt coming from the piece when she had held it in her hands now seemed to envelop her, created by the anxious energy of those around her.

The Sand God lifted his hands and the pieces flew toward him as if attached to his palms by invisible strings. The shards spun faster and faster, until they appeared to be a single object. The Sand God closed his hands around the spinning light, and when he opened them, he was holding a beautiful gem—a brilliant blue star-shaped sapphire.

The Sand God bent down, holding the gem out to Jasmine. "Take better care of it this time," he said, his voice a mix of wind and thunder.

"We will," promised Jasmine. "Thank—"

The Sand God did not wait for her to finish. As he straightened up, he transformed again into a tornado of sand and then burst apart into millions of magical twinkling grains, which scattered across the desert floor.

"He's such a show-off," muttered Turab.

Jasmine glanced into the distance. "The sandstorms are gone!" she said. The others followed her gaze. The sky was clear as far as they could see. The stars, which had been hidden behind dust for days, now twinkled brightly.

Layli felt a tingle move through her body and she knew she had her magic back. Within seconds, she had returned to her gulin form.

"Layli!" Bedair rushed to her and the two gulin hugged.

"I could go for a nice slice of walnut cake right about now," said Genie. He snapped his fingers and held out his hand. The sticky treat instantly appeared in his palm. "Yes!" he shouted. "I'm *baaaaaack*, baby!"

A moment later, a familiar form sailed over the walls of Agrabah toward them.

Aladdin waved. "Carpet!" he called out.

"That's *Magic* Carpet to you," said Genie jokingly as Magic Carpet sailed gracefully down to the crowd. Carpet flicked out a tassel and playfully slapped Aladdin's open palm. Then he floated to the ground, allowing Jasmine and Aladdin to climb on, along with Genie and Abu.

Jasmine gestured to Turab to come aboard as well.

"No thanks," said Turab. "Seeing you all work together makes me realize how lonely I was in there." He gestured to the tunnel opening. "I never really mixed with the other magic guardian types. But now I think I might reach out, make some connections. See what it's like to have—" he glanced around at the crowd—"friends." He smiled and cast his arms open wide, exploding into bits of clay and dirt. The others ducked and darted out of the way as the clumps sailed off as if propelled by a breeze.

"We're ready," Jasmine said to Magic Carpet. "Let's go!" Magic Carpet rose into the air. "Come with us!" Jasmine called back to the gulin as the carpet headed for Agrabah.

Umab waved to the gulin crowd. "Come, gulin! Let us sail alongside Magic Carpet—and meet our friends in Agrabah!" Umab's shape-shifting ability had been restored, and she transformed into an owl. She hooted, urging the hesitant gulin to follow her lead. At last they obeyed, becoming parrots and partridges, pigeons and doves.

Layli and Bedair didn't need to be asked twice.

They had already shape-shifted into eagles and caught up with Magic Carpet. The flock of green-tinged birds soon followed, Umab hooting at the front, all of them now eager and excited to see the sapphire—and peace between humans and gulin—restored.

CHAPTER 21

At dawn the next morning, members of the royal guard removed the clay star from the arch in the city gates and replaced it with the original, repaired gem. It was a beautiful, clear day, and the restored sapphire twinkled and gleamed in the warm sunshine. Jasmine and her friends stood below with the Sultan, Umab, and the gulin. A few residents of the city had ventured out as well. They all stared up at the sapphire, overwhelmed by the sight.

"The storms may be over," the Sultan told the crowd. "But our work has only begun."

Over the next several hours, the people of Agrabah, assisted by the royal guards, worked together to sweep the sand from the streets and repair the buildings damaged by the storms. In the marketplace, Umab led the gulin in offering assistance. The gulin were still shy, and many of the humans remained wary as well. Layli did her best to inspire playfulness on both sides.

"Follow my lead," Layli whispered to a nearby gulin. Layli shape-shifted into a squirrel and borrowed a shelled almond from a vendor cart. The other gulin shape-shifted as well. Layli tossed her the almond, and the two green-furred squirrels embarked on a lively game of catch. Humans and gulin paused in their work to watch and laugh.

Umab spotted the hijinks. "*Layli.*" She frowned in disapproval. The squirrels froze. Umab's scowl dissolved into a smile. "Just joking!" she said with a laugh. "Carry on."

A few other gulin tentatively joined in. One shape-shifted into a dove and tickled a woman's cheek with a feathered wing. Another became a gerbil and skittered up to a little boy, who shrieked with glee as he scooped up the tiny creature in his hands. Soon all the gulin were taking part in the fun, spicing up the crowd's labors with moments of joy.

Meanwhile, Umab had made her way to Jasmine and the Sultan, who had arrived at the marketplace to offer encouragement and a helping hand. Jasmine had briefly introduced her father to the gulin leader the night before. Umab addressed the Sultan. "I would very much like to take Your Highness on a tour of our homes in the tunnels after they have been repaired," she said.

"I would be honored," replied the Sultan. "On the condition that you allow our guards to help with those repairs, and that you and the other gulin consider the streets of Agrabah to be your home as well." Umab nodded in thanks.

Jasmine had spotted Aladdin, with Abu on his shoulder, approaching the market on his crutches, and she hurried over to him. "How did it go?" she asked.

Aladdin and Genie had taken Rula and Nabil back to Qamar to ask the magic glass collector to check the weather in the other locations throughout the kingdom. "All clear everywhere," reported Aladdin, who had returned to Agrabah on Magic Carpet.

"And Genie has resumed his travels?" asked Jasmine.

Aladdin raised the flap on the satchel he was carrying on his shoulder. "Let's see, shall we?" he said with a grin. He took out one of Qamar's magic frames and tapped on the red opal on the corner. A moment later, Genie appeared in the glass.

"Genie!" cried Jasmine.

"Princess! Check it out! Glitz and glimmer for days." Genie shifted the frame to reveal a huge bazaar spread out across a large city square. Rows of tables displayed antique objects of all types, which sparkled in the bright sunshine. "Qamar gave me a tip on this annual antiques market in the north. I'm getting some *amazing* deals."

"Who are you speaking to?" called a voice near Genie. "Is that picture in your frame *moving*?"

Genie tilted the glass toward a perplexed antiques vendor with a long gray beard. "Say hello to Princess Jasmine of Agrabah."

The elderly vendor stared into the glass in shock. "Uh . . . Your Highness . . . I . . . uh—"

The view whipped back to Genie. "Gotta get back to haggling. I'll come visit soon." Genie snapped his fingers and several gold coins appeared in his hand. He winked into the frame. "Tell Layli and Bedair I'll pick them up a shiny goody or two."

The image went dark. "Back to his old tricks," Aladdin said to Jasmine with a laugh.

Jasmine smiled. "I'm happy to see that."

Bedair, in his human form, emerged from

the tunnel entrance they had gone into the night before.

"Where have you been?" Jasmine asked him. "You missed seeing your friends rediscover the fun of shape-shifting."

Bedair glanced over Jasmine's shoulder and smiled as he watched a small fox with green flecks in its red fur run circles around an exasperated guard's ankles. "I hope there will be plenty more pranks to see in the future," he said. He turned to Aladdin. "You've seemed so familiar to me, ever since we met in the desert. I brought this from my cave to show you." He held out a framed drawing of two young men, their arms slung around each other, grinning. One was Bedair and the other seemed to be . . .

"That's you!" Jasmine said to Aladdin.

"Only if he were over a thousand years old," said Bedair. "No, this is my dear old friend Niddal. This drawing was done back before the sapphire broke."

Abu leapt onto Bedair's shoulder to peer closer at the drawing.

"Wow," said Aladdin. "So this could be my great-great—however many *greats* there are in a thousand years—grandfather?"

The three studied the drawing. "It *does* seem possible," said Jasmine.

"If not for your ankle, we could race to the gates," said Bedair. "If you lost, that would *prove* you're related to Niddal. He could never beat me in anything."

Aladdin narrowed his eyes at the challenge. Abu hopped back to Aladdin's shoulder and whispered in his ear. "Good idea," said Aladdin. He turned to Bedair. "How about a juggling contest? We can both sit to make it even."

"You've never seen me juggle, friend," warned Bedair.

"You've never seen *me* juggle," replied Aladdin. "Go get two chairs and a dozen onions."

"*Apricots*," suggested Bedair.

"Messy!" exclaimed Aladdin. "I love it!"

Jasmine laughed, amused but also pleased at the friendship that was forming in front of her. "I'd stay and cheer you on," she told Aladdin, "but I have a feeling this is only the first competition that's going to occur between you two."

The Sultan had approached and overheard the last of the conversation. "Whatever you do, no racing up to the sapphire," he warned the two new friends.

"I promise," Aladdin and Bedair replied in unison.

The Sultan and Jasmine returned to the market, where several stalls had opened for business. "It's wonderful to see things getting back to normal," Jasmine told her father.

"And yet much has changed," replied the Sultan, with a sidelong glance to his daughter. "You have done a great, brave thing, my child."

"Thank you." Jasmine was reluctant to dampen her father's respect, but she needed to be honest with him. "I had such doubts, though," she said. "When things went right, I would feel confident for a moment, but when a new problem arose, the fear that I might not be able to overcome it would return. It was all I could do to keep going." She shook her head with dismay. "I worry I will always have doubts."

"Oh, my dear daughter," said the Sultan, grasping Jasmine's hands. "Do you truly believe I never have doubts?" He smiled at Jasmine's look of surprise. "They say wisdom comes from experience, but wisdom does not mean you have all the answers. What experience teaches you is that doubts are a part of the process. And that the unknown and the unexpected are always lurking around the corner, ready to test you, again and again. You *did* keep going, despite your doubts, and *that* is what makes you the kind of leader Agrabah needs."

Warmed by her father's words, Jasmine took in the sights around her. Gulin laughing and chatting with humans. Vendors haggling with buyers. Layli in human form, biting into a fresh plum, eyes wide with delight. Aladdin and Bedair facing off against each other, apricots in hand as Abu looked on from a window ledge. The old way of life and the new, blending together into a better present.

Jasmine realized there was one thing she never had to doubt about herself: no matter what lay ahead, she would always do everything she could to ensure the happiness of everyone in the kingdom. *That,* she believed, was the most important leadership skill of all.

Ready for more original adventures starring your favorite Disney princesses?